THE BATTLE FOR VICTORIA STREET

GABIANN MARIN

Omnibus Books
An imprint of Scholastic Australia Pty Limited (ABN 11 000 614 577)
PO Box 579 Gosford NSW 2250
www.scholastic.com.au

Part of the Scholastic Group
Sydney • Auckland • New York • Toronto • London • Mexico City • New Delhi
Hong Kong • Buenos Aires • Puerto Rico

Published by Omnibus Books in 2024.

Cover and internals designed by Laura Ye.

A catalogue record for this book is available from the National Library of Australia

ISBN: 978-1-74383-399-5

Typeset in Arno Pro Regular.

Printed in China by RR Donnelley.
Scholastic Australia's policy, in association with RR Donnelley, is to use papers that are renewable and made efficiently from wood grown in responsibly managed forests, so as to minimise its environmental footprint.

24 25 26 27 28 / 2

THE BATTLE FOR VICTORIA STREET

GABIANN MARIN

An Omnibus Book from Scholastic Australia

This book is dedicated to my mother, Jeni; the inspiration for the fictional mother in this novel.

Thank you for being extraordinary, generous and brave, and for following your own unconventional path. But mostly thank you for loving books and encouraging me to write them. None of the good things in my life would have ever happened without you. I am proud to be your daughter.

1 JANUARY 1973

It's the first day of the New Year and I am eleven years old today!

It's great being born on New Year's Day because everyone celebrates my birthday with fireworks and big parties. I like the Catherine wheel and the bangers the best. Ma even lets me and Darren light up the Roman candles—but we have to be careful because a few years ago a boy in our street was mucking about with firecrackers and almost lost an eye.

Mrs Fowler, who is the neighbour down the road and is really, really old, gave me this diary for my birthday. She reckons it's important for us to write down what happens every day. She calls it a 'social history'.

She showed me some old diaries and said that long after the writers died, historians read those diaries and stuff to know what life was like back then. I reckon she's right, too. At school, Mrs Frater, my teacher, is always telling us about all these old people who were really important.

Some of it is dead boring, to be honest, but I like the idea that one day, far in the future, a bunch of kids in a classroom might read this diary and think I was a really cool sheila.

So, I guess I should start my diary by introducing myself.

My name's Billie. Well, my actual name is Wilomena Anastasia Krum, but who can get their mouth around that! So everyone just calls me Billie. Everyone except my pa, who insists on using my full name because I was named after him and he thinks it's important I don't forget it. Honestly, that ridiculous name is the only thing my pa ever gave me. And I hate it. Which makes sense if you know my father. He never was one to give anyone anything but trouble.

He's gone now. Not dead or anything, just moved out years ago. Left me and my ma and my brother Darren all alone in our basement flat at 85 Victoria Street. Ma says I was born in that basement, but not my brother Darren, who was born in the hospital up on Oxford Street. I think being born here makes me belong to the house somehow, and it belong to me, even though we don't own it. We just rent a room, like the other people who live in the building.

We don't live in the basement anymore. Ma moved us up to the top floor as soon as she could afford it because the basement is really dark and mouldy. When we moved upstairs, Ma was so excited. She said we were moving up in the world! I love our big room because it is light and bright and has a window that looks across Sydney Harbour. I spend a lot of my time when I'm stuck indoors just staring out that window, looking at the ferries and the bridge and watching the Sydney Opera House being built. It's the weirdest shape you've ever seen. Ma says it will look more like a normal building once all the scaffolding comes off, but I don't think it will.

Don't get me wrong, I don't spend much time indoors at all. I am out on the street with my mates every chance I get. Victoria Street is a great place to just hang around and play jump rope or kick the can or watch the weird and wonderful people go by.

The street is always full of people—artists and factory workers, families and old ladies, all living side by side. The long-haired hippies sit on balconies playing out-of-tune guitars, and glamorous lemon-haired ladies click up the asphalt in heels so high I don't know how they stay upright.

Victoria Street is a crossroads, like in those old stories of bushrangers and highwaymen. It's a place where everyone and everything crosses paths. It's wedged between Kings Cross with its pubs and clubs and tourists on one side, and a sheer cliff drop into Woolloomooloo on the other.

To get into Victoria Street, you have to cross busy Darlinghurst Road, fighting through traffic and never-ending roadworks on William Street, ignoring the angry, red-faced drivers trying to make their way to or from the city.

At the other end of the street, the Cross runs into Potts Point, which is hilly and quiet and looks out across the shores of the sprawling Sydney Harbour. The harbour is full of grey, shadowy naval ships and bright, happy ferries scurrying under that big metal coat hanger that spans the water.

And sitting right smack in the middle of all this is Victoria Street. A street right out of a fairytale, I reckon.

We even have a witch who lives just up the laneway and an heiress who lives a few doors down. Her name is Miss Jane and you can see her most days sitting on the dirty front steps of her house, looking like a fairy princess in her silk dresses. Often she's delivering letters and flyers or holding street rallies, surrounded by loads of people all cheering and yelling.

And all up and down the street are the castles. Well, they aren't really castles, just huge old houses filled with laughter, songs, yelling, mould and dust, but they are the closest thing to castles I have ever seen in real life. They are all big and grand, but none of them are exactly alike, like brothers and sisters from the same family. Each of them has their own personality, too. Some are large and spooky, others are bright and cheerful, some are crumbling and derelict. Some have open front lawns; others have doors opening right onto the street. Behind the houses are rows of back alleys and dunny lanes where all of us kids play hide-and-seek or street cricket.

And all of it belongs together somehow, like the same people made them all, even if they did it in different ways and at different times.

But it's not the houses I really notice when I walk along Victoria Street. It's the trees. Huge, they are, taller than most of the houses, and they go all the way down both sides of the street, making the whole place look like a river of green in spring and summer and a carpet of golden leaves in autumn. It seems so strange to have a street like this right in the middle of Darlinghurst, with all the clubs and shops and the tourists. But here it is.

That's what is so great about this place. Here, everything and everyone belongs. Even me, a scruffy eleven-year-old girl in pink overalls, with a gap in my teeth and hair that's too curly and tangled to ever stay in plaits.

2 JANUARY 1973

Victoria Street is usually a quiet place, even though it's set right where the suburbs of Darlinghurst, Woolloomooloo and Kings Cross meet. Of course, we don't call any of them their long names. Woolloomooloo is just called the Loo, Darlinghurst is Darlo and Kings Cross . . . well, it gets called all sorts of things. But we kids mostly call it the Strip because that's what all the locals call it.

But things have changed. People here used to be more friendly. Even though there were lots of people coming and going in the flats and rooms of the boarding houses, a lot of us have been here for a very long time and are good friends. Now, lots of the neighbours I knew have moved away. And the others aren't quite so friendly. Ma hardly ever stops in the street to chat to people and there are a lot more strangers in the street now, too. Not just the tourists or backpackers staying a few weeks in the boarding houses across the road, or noisy groups of people wandering in from the Cross as they try to find their way home after a big night out. These strangers are different. Mean-looking men with handlebar moustaches and bright fluro-coloured tracksuits. The kind of men you only ever used to see up near the clubs and tattoo parlours on Darlo Road. They don't live here, just stroll in and stand around in the shade of the trees, watching people who aren't doing much of anything, and acting like they own the place even though I know they don't. Ma says I must stay away from them and never speak to them, even if they try to speak to me.

My neighbours are getting a bit strange, too, staying indoors more often, so it's quieter on the street than it has ever been before. Ma always says that just before a big storm hits, the world goes still and quiet. I can't help but think maybe there is a storm coming, a big one. Not like a regular storm, with rain and hail, but a different kind of storm, like something bad is going to happen.

Maybe I'm just imagining it because of all the problems down in the Loo. There is a lot of trouble down there, with noisy protests all the time and bulldozers turning up and knocking down houses, some with people still living in them. Loads of people have been arrested, but still more people turn up and stand in front of the bulldozers and the cranes, yelling at the coppers who are always trying to move them on.

I don't understand what the people in the Loo have done to make those in charge so angry that they are taking their homes away. Ma says the people haven't done anything. But the government, who owns all those houses, wants to sell them to a company who wants to turn it all into a big old road right down to the harbour.

I have to pass the construction sites every morning and

afternoon on my way to school. Ma has made me promise not to go into the sites because she thinks I might get run over by a bulldozer or something, or that Darren might wander in and get hurt if I'm not watching. I don't want to go too close anyway because it's really noisy and dusty. Although once, when the bulldozers first started, I did go over to have a quick squizz. A big wrecking ball slammed right into the wall of a house and brought it down, even as the people who lived in the house were standing in the street yelling for them to stop. There was furniture and toys and everything still inside, and it all just fell into the rubble and was pushed into piles by the bulldozers or scooped up and dumped by the front-end loaders. It was after that house came down that all the protesters turned up. They make it much harder for the bulldozers and cranes and wrecking balls, but a lot of the houses have come down anyway and some areas are completely flattened now.

I heard Ma talking with our neighbour Mrs Gatto about it and they were both worried that the bulldozers could come up here next and knock all our houses down. But we are right on the top of a cliff, so I don't think the bulldozers could get up here. It's way too steep.

Anyway, our landlord Mr Carson, owns most of the

houses up here and even though I've never met him, I don't think he would want to do anything bad to our house. It's wrong to do that to people and take away their homes, everyone knows that. I think I would join the protesters if they tried anything up here. That's if Ma would let me.

Ma and Mrs Gatto don't like our landlord. They call him a slumlord and say all he cares about is money. But when I asked what a slumlord was, no-one would tell me. I think it must be a curse word, so I am going to ask my friend Jacko because he knows what all the worst words mean.

5 JANUARY 1973

I visited our neighbour Mrs Fowler today.

She lives up the street at number 115, near the Butler Stairs, in a flat she shares with her son Mick, who is almost always travelling on the sea.

Ma likes me to take Darren up there when Mick is away. Otherwise, Mrs Fowler is all on her own and she's too old and frail to get out much.

I don't mind. I like Mrs Fowler. Her flat is always so neat.

She has lots of cool stuff like old clocks and stuffed animals under big glass jars. And the whole place always smells nice, like lilac and talcum powder. Whenever we visit, Mrs Fowler gives Darren Iced VoVo biscuits and lets me drink tea out of a proper teacup with a saucer. I almost never spill it.

Mrs Fowler seems pretty posh for someone on Vic Street. Most of us just wear jeans and T-shirts, hand-me-downs or homemade clothes. But Mrs Fowler always dresses really elegantly in white frilly blouses, or heavy woollen dresses in winter, with a dead fox scarf wrapped around her neck if she is going out.

There are five flats where Mrs Fowler lives, but she says it was once a stately home for just one family.

I reckon the posh people who used to live here didn't like to wash much or they would have put in better bathrooms! Most of the people on our street, including Mrs Fowler, don't even have proper inside dunnies.

But Mrs Fowler said that they didn't have plumbing or running water or anything back then, it was all added after the posh people had moved out.

We didn't have a proper inside flushing toilet at our place either, until Mr Gatto put one in. He knows how to do plumbing and stuff. My friend Susie thinks we are so lucky to have a proper inside toilet, but I would swap it for her black-and-white TV any day.

Still, I reckon all up my flat in number 85 is a pretty great place to live, even if it isn't as big and grand as some of the other houses on the street. Sure, there are wet patches of mould on most of the walls and in both the bathrooms, and the paint peels off in soft, thick flakes no matter how often Mr Gatto repaints it—but so what!

I really like all the people who live in our house, which is split up into five different flats in the main house and a basement flat below. There is Mr Ted, who lives in the front downstairs flat. He's a bit old and deaf and is always yelling because he can't hear what you say to him. I don't know why he thinks yelling makes us sound any louder, but yell he does, and we yell right back.

The Finnegans, who live in the upstairs room across from us, are originally from a place called Ireland. They have five kids all crammed in the one room, but their room is double the size of ours. And it's three times as big as the tiny back room on the ground floor behind the kitchen, where Mr Lionel lives. He always says as long as there is enough room for him, his books and his typewriter, he's happy.

Miss Maggie and Miss Maude moved into the basement

flat after we moved upstairs. They are both dancers and they look like sisters, but Ma says they aren't. They fill the house with music and movement and teach me how to dance.

Mr and Mrs Gatto and their sons have the only other rooms in the house—the big flat on the bottom left of the ground floor. It is two rooms instead of one and is by far the biggest flat in the house. They need all that room, though, because the Gattos are big, happy people with four boys. There's their eldest son John, who works as a butcher's apprentice, the twins Benny and Al, who just graduated from high school, and Tony. He's only a year older than me and is one of my best mates.

Tony told me once that Gatto was Italian for cat, so I call him Tony the Cat. He pretends he doesn't like the nickname, but I know he does because I heard him introducing himself as Tony the Cat to some of the older boys down at the arcade.

They also had another son, Ernesto, but he died in the war in South-East Asia when I was little and I don't remember ever meeting him. I know what he looked like, though, because the Gattos keep a framed photograph of him in military uniform in the front room, right next to their big wooden crucifix.

Tony the Cat is one of my mates in my gang, along with Jacko, my best mate Susie and Darren. We call ourselves the

Vic Street gang because we all live on Victoria Street. Any kid who lives on this street can join our group. We often have a few others who live on surrounding streets, like Challis Avenue, hang around with us as well. But only the five of us are the proper, original Vic Street gang kids.

Jacko is the oldest member of the Vic Street gang; he's turning thirteen years old in March and he's going to high school this year. Tony, Susie and I are all in Grade Five, even though Tony is a year older than us girls. He got held back at school because he misses so many days helping his dad out at their fish shop. Darren is the youngest in our gang, so we all make sure to look out for him.

That's the thing about Victoria Street—we all look out for each other. You have to, my Ma says, because no-one gets through this world all on their own.

10 JANUARY 1973

Ma isn't home yet and Darren is in bed, so I am in charge.

Ma works really hard down at Harry's Café de Wheels, which is a pie shop on Cowper Bay Road. Well, it's not so much a shop as a caravan that sits on the sidewalk down by the harbour. She says she was lucky to get that job because famous people from all over the world come to buy a pie at Harry's and eat it standing by the trailer, looking out at the water. The manager even has a photo of Colonel Sanders eating a Harry's pie, which he said was better than his own Kentucky Fried Chicken recipe.

I don't like the pies all that much, to be honest, because they put yukky green goo on the top of them and they have a lot of pepper in the meat. But don't let Ma know because she almost always brings the leftovers home and I pretend I like them for her sake. She's always really tired when she finishes work and I know she is happy not to have to cook us anything in the downstairs kitchen. If we have pies there's never any washing up for me to do either, so I can put up with the gluggy, cold, peppery taste.

Ma mostly works day shifts while we're at school, but sometimes she has to work nights and weekends and almost every school holiday. I try to help out where I can by looking after Darren and doing the laundry or the mending. I also make sure to pick up all our clothes and toys so Ma doesn't fall over them when she comes home.

My brother Darren is seven years old now and he's a really

good brother. I don't mind looking after him at all, although sometimes he does get into a bit of trouble. But you can't stay cross with Darren. He's really the sweetest kid and loves everyone and everything. Darren was born with Down syndrome, which means I have to be extra careful to watch out for him because sometimes he doesn't understand things as quickly as I do.

I know Ma feels bad for working so much, but me and Darren are all right, really. When Ma's working nights, Mrs Gatto lets us eat with them and hang out in their flat till Ma gets home. Mrs Gatto cooks the best Italian food and I like it way more than the pies.

Oh, I hear Ma coming home. I best go see if there are any pies that need putting in the ice box.

14 JANUARY 1973

There was a big rally on our street today. A tall, red-headed woman was talking on a loudspeaker and lots of people were standing around listening to her. She said that Mr Carson wants to turn our street into a carpark! And all the houses from numbers 55 to 115 are going to be knocked down if we don't stop it somehow. That includes my house!

I ran home and told Mrs Gatto and Ma and some of the others who were all sitting in the kitchen having a cup of tea. None of them looked even a bit surprised.

I had the flyer that one of the people at the rally was handing out, so I know there is a big meeting for all the people on our street who want to stand against Mr Carson's plans. But Ma said I couldn't go because those meetings could get dangerous. Mrs Gatto said the same thing. Mr Lionel said he had gone to one a few weeks back and the cops had come and arrested almost everyone and the thugs and goons on the street had made threats to those who weren't arrested.

I can't believe they all knew about this and didn't tell me. But Ma said that Mr Carson doesn't have permission to do anything yet and if we all just go about our business like we normally do and not cause trouble, the whole thing will probably blow over.

I don't believe her, though, and neither does Tony the Cat. He agrees with me that we should get the Vic Street gang together and do what we can to protect our street.

26 JANUARY 1973

It's Australia Day today and everyone gets to have a long weekend to celebrate the First Fleet bringing all the people over from England and establishing the colony of New South Wales. Those old ships landed right down on the harbour below us and the sailors and the convicts set up camps and tents and stuff on the beach, probably just near where Circular Quay is now.

Loads of people are running around Kings Cross and down at the harbour, waving tiny Australian flags and singing 'God Save the Queen', which is our National Anthem, though I can't see how it has anything to do with Australia, really. It all seems to be about Queen Elizabeth and how she's in danger and we have to rescue her, which makes zero sense because as far as I know the Queen is nice and safe in her home in Buckingham Palace all the way over in England.

Our prime minster Mr Whitlam doesn't think much of the National Anthem either, because he announced a big competition where you could write a new Australian National Anthem and if he liked it, you would win $500 and get your song as the official national song of Australia.

My best friend Susie and I started writing one.

This is what we came up with:

Koalas, kangaroos,
Australia is full of them.
We have meat pies, barbeques,
with tomato sauce on all of them.
Everyone we know
thinks Australia's pretty great.
So, if you don't agree,
you can rack off with all your mates.

I think it's pretty good, though we only have the one verse and 'God Save the Queen' has six verses, so we have to work on it a bit more. But we've got a few weeks until the deadline and I think we will make it pretty bonza by then. I am already thinking about how I might spend my half of the $500 prize money.

People on our street really get into Australia Day. Almost every house has an Australian flag in the window, although some of the houses down in the Loo have a different flag. It's black and red with a big yellow circle in the middle of it. I liked the look of it but neither Susie or I knew what it was for, so we decided to visit Donnie McLaren because his house in the Loo is one that has that new flag flying.

Donnie goes to Plunket Street Public School, same as

us, so we know him pretty well, even though he isn't a Vic Street kid. I think he was surprised when Susie and I turned up asking about his flag. He didn't mind, though, and told us all about it. It's the Aboriginal flag, meant to represent people like Donnie who were here before the white Europeans came to Australia. Donnie reckons a lot of the Aboriginal people don't like celebrating Australia Day because that was the day that they lost their lands to the Europeans. So, they are flying this flag on Australia Day to remind us all that this place was not empty land when Captain Cook came and he didn't discover it, just found it after the Aboriginal people had been here for thousands of years.

Donnie's dad heard us all talking and he came and gave us tea and told us that in his culture the land is home and you belong to it, not the other way around. Owning land and making money from it is a European idea, he said. Before that, the Aboriginal people thought of the land as a living thing that they helped to look after and, in return, it provided them with food and shelter. Before the Europeans came, the Aboriginal people had never heard of landlords or rents or any of that stuff. He said now the people who owned the land had all the power and the people who just lived on it had none. Even if they had lived here for years and the land held their stories and the stories of their ancestors, those with power could just take it all away. That meant that most people would never know what it was like to be part of the place where they lived.

I asked Donnie's dad why we hadn't seen this flag last Australia Day and he said it has only been around for a little while. A man named Harold Thomas designed it in 1971, but it wasn't until the Aboriginal Embassy was set up in 1972 that it became the official flag for Aboriginal Australians.

I could see Donnie was really proud of his flag. While we were there, the coppers came around and told his family and their neighbours to stop waving it around because it wasn't the proper official flag of the Queen and stuff.

I'm glad Donnie's family didn't take it down, though. It isn't hurting anyone.

18 FEBRUARY 1973

Holidays are over and it's back to school next week. I'm going to miss having all day free to spend with my mates.

Jacko, Susie, Darren and I mostly spent the holidays

playing cricket or collecting tinnie rings. The streets are always littered with the rings which people pull off their tinnies and just drop on the ground. They can be sharp as razors those pull rings, so you have to be careful picking them up in case you cut your fingers. It's worth a few cuts, though, because they make really cool jewellery which Susie and I wear or give as presents to our mums for Mother's Day.

I think my ma really likes them because she always puts them in a special box and never wears them out. She says they will make the other women on the street jealous that they don't have jewellery as nice as the pull ring ones I make her.

I don't really mind going back to school. I like Plunkett Street mostly, even though it takes about twenty minutes to walk down one of the staircases from Vic Street to school and a bit longer coming back. If I didn't have to always wait for Darren, I reckon I could do it in fifteen minutes each way, though.

Plunkett Street is the closest school to us Vic Street kids, except for the posh private school at the end of our street. I don't like the girls who go there. They always have perfectly straight hair and wear a uniform that makes them all look almost the same, with a stupid little straw hat and perfectly shiny black leather shoes. They are always saying mean things to us Vic Street kids and acting like they are so much better than we are.

I like that Plunkett Street doesn't have a uniform. We all wear whatever we want, although Ma always insists Darren and I wear proper black shoes to school even though loads of the other kids mostly wear thongs and many of them don't wear any shoes at all.

Ma says that's because their families can't afford to give them proper shoes. But I don't understand that because we are poor, too. We get our clothes mostly from the Wayside Chapel charity drive or hand-me-downs from other kids in our street who have grown out of them. Yet somehow Ma always manages to find the ugliest brown or black shoes every time we grow out of the last pair.

I hate wearing any shoes, but I hate those ones most of all because they never fit right and always leave blisters unless I wear socks. Last year, I gave my shoes to one of the girls in Grade Three who didn't have any and Ma was so mad when I came home without them, she made me go right up to the girl's house and ask for them back. It was so embarrassing! That girl is gone now. She lived in one of the first houses that got knocked down in the Loo and had to move away, so I guess if she had kept my shoes they might be buried under a pile of rubble where her house used to be. Instead, I have to keep wearing them, even though they are getting really tight around my toes now.

I've grown a lot since last year, so most of my clothes, as well as the shoes, really don't fit me very well anymore. Ma says we'll go to Wayside for their Easter jumble sale and get me a new dress. I hope it has flowers on it. Susie got one with flowers on it last year and she always looks so pretty in it. I got a dirty brown one, with ruffles around the edges and purple ribbon which is faded and fraying at the hem. It's awful so I don't wear it very much. Mostly I wear my overalls and one of my T-shirts, with a green cardigan if it's cold, but if that gets too dirty, I have to wear the ugly dress.

This year, I am starting Grade Five at Plunkett Street, which means a shared class with the Grade Six kids. The big old building where I go to school doesn't have enough rooms for every grade to have its own classroom and there are loads of Grade Fours taking up the other rooms and only a few of us in Grade Five. The school is really old. A sign over the door says it was opened in the 1800s, so I guess there were less kids around then and they didn't need as much room.

Now, though, the school is packed with kids from Darlinghurst, the Loo and some from Potts Point. They keep saying they are going to make the place bigger. There are three demountables out on what used to be the playground, but they are even worse to sit in than the classrooms in the big building because they are made entirely of metal and on a hot day it's like being inside an oven. I was in one all through Grade Four and I really hope our Grade Five class is in the proper building this year.

Darren isn't old enough to go to Plunkett Street Primary yet, so I drop him off at the infant school on the way—it's only across the road from us, in a building not nearly as old as ours. I sort of miss being in infant school. It was nice there because the rooms are bigger and they have books and toys in every room, not just the library. I know I am too old for toys now, but I did like the Snoopy doll they used to let you take home over the weekend if you did the best on the spelling test. Darren never gets to take it home, which I think is unfair, because they make the words much too hard to spell now.

They also give the infants kids free lunches: salad rolls in summer, and soup or sometimes a sausage roll in winter. And free milk in little bottles which they always left sitting stacked up in the playground until lunchtime so when we opened them, they were warm and tasted kind of off. They stopped giving out free lunches at the primary school a few years back so now if I want a school lunch, I have to pay ten cents for it. Which is a complete rip off if you ask me! They do still have free milk in primary, but me, I'd rather drink water than that stuff, so I mostly drink from the school bubbler.

Sometimes Ma gives me money for the school lunch, but mostly I have to make do with a tomato sauce sandwich, or a cold pie if there are any left over from the ones Ma brings home from Harry's. It's not much, but I don't complain because it's better than nothing, which is what a lot of the Loo kids get.

I'm not trying to be mean about the Loo kids. It's not their fault they can't afford anything. Everyone who goes to Plunkett Street is poor, it's just that the Loo kids are a bit poorer than the rest of us. They are okay, though, and I get on with most of them. It's the mean kids who have been held back in Grades 5 and 6 who I don't like. They bully the younger kids into giving up their lunches or lunch money. You have to make sure you avoid those kids as much as possible because they can get really rough if you don't. Most of them don't pick on us Vic Street kids because we stick together and they know it's easier to pick on the kids who are on their own.

The only one I ever really have to worry about is Tommo Jenkins. He's the biggest kid at the school because he's been held back twice in Grade Five, which means if he is held back again, he'll be in my class for sure. He is the meanest kid I know, so it's a good thing he hardly ever turns up to school. When he does attend, you've got to watch out for him because he'll come after anyone, even people who don't have any lunch money he can steal.

The best teacher at Plunkett Street is Mrs Frater. I had her last year and she said I was a really smart kid. She's really nice and has hair so long that even when it's plaited in one long, thick braid, it reaches almost down to the small of her back. I hope she takes us again this year. She could because she often swaps between taking the fourth and fifth grade with Mrs Garth.

I hate Mrs Garth. She is a mean rissole with a bad temper and a face that always looks cranky.

I've never been in her class, but my mate Jacko had her two years running. He told us how she would sneak up behind the kids as they were filling in their form books and if she saw any wrong answers, she would hit the poor miserable kid really hard with her ruler right across their knuckles and call them stupid.

'You never saw her coming,' Jacko would say. 'So, you spent the whole class terrified she would suddenly appear behind you and slap you with that heavy wooden stick!'

It will be a terrible year if I end up in a class with both Tommo Jenkins and Mrs Garth!

20 FEBRUARY 1973

Mrs Frater is taking our class. I was so relieved to see her there when we walked in, I hugged her. She was cool about it because she knows me from last year. A lot of the other kids hugged her, too. I reckon we are all really pleased not to get Mrs Garth, though I feel sorry for those poor fourth graders who are stuck with her.

I showed Mrs Frater this journal and all the stuff I had written in it. I reckon she was really impressed. She even said I could use it as part of our new history assignment, which is a task to find out the history of our suburb and write about the big changes that have happened over the last hundred years or so. She said we were living at a time in history where things were changing really fast.

A lot of the kids don't like this new assignment because they think history is boring, but I love history. I love all those stories of people who lived before and all the beautiful old things they made and kept for us which we can use now. If it wasn't for people in the past, I wouldn't have any of my favourite clothes or the pink and white music box that Mrs Fowler gave me last Christmas, which she said was made way back in the last century!

Mrs Frater agrees with me.

When she was talking about the assignment, she said, 'Those who don't know about the past are destined to repeat it.'

I didn't quite understand what that meant, but I think it sounds cool. She explained it meant that through looking at what had happened in the past, and the mistakes that were made, we could avoid making those mistakes again and live better, happier lives than the people who came before us. I like this idea because I make enough of my own mistakes without repeating theirs!

Mrs Frater said she was giving us this assignment because our suburbs—the Loo and Darlinghurst—were being considered for something called heritage status. This means that a lot of important people are choosing some of the most important buildings and areas in the whole of NSW to keep safe from development and demolition. If we can show that where we live has important historical value—like famous people lived there or important events happened or the buildings are unique in some way—then our suburbs may get on these lists.

I am very excited about this because if we can show people how important Victoria Street is, then no-one will want to turn it into a carpark and me and Darren and Ma won't have to move away.

Mrs Frater said if our history reports were good enough, she would include them in a letter she is sending to the heritage people. So I am going to work really hard on making my report extra good.

23 FEBRUARY 1973

Susie and I visited Mrs Fowler after school today and asked her to help us with our history project. Mrs Fowler is the oldest person I know, so I reckon she will know all about history and stuff. She seemed really pleased we were doing it on Victoria Street and said we could come by tomorrow and she would give us tea and cakes and answer all our questions.

24 FEBRUARY 1973

Today Mrs Fowler showed us an old picture of farmland and windmills. I didn't know what it was at first, then I realised that the windmills were sitting along Sydney Harbour. That was what Cowper's Bay Wharf looked like back in the early 1800s! Mrs Fowler said it was no wonder that I didn't recognise it because it was very different to today. And all those windmills pumped water and made electricity for all the people in the Sydney colony, way back before they knew how to build power stations.

Our suburb was just a big meadow back then, it wasn't even called Darlinghurst. The whole area from the Cross to the harbour was called Henrietta Town after our first governor, Governor Macquarie's wife, Henrietta. The name changed in the 1820s when the next governor, a man named Ralph Darling, decided to name the place after his wife, Eliza. He didn't call it Eliza Town, he called it Darlinghurst, which was his last name, so it sounds more like he was naming it after him than honouring her, if you ask me.

Back when Ralph and Eliza were around, there wasn't a Victoria Street like there is today. In fact, there weren't any real roads at all. Just seventeen huge estates that owned all the land between them. Mrs Fowler said the fanciest people in Sydney lived right here and it was the place to come for dances and fancy parties.

I asked Mrs Fowler if that was what it was like when she was our age. She laughed and said even though she may look old, she wasn't quite 150 years old just yet!

But she did know that in the 1850s the estates were sold off and Woolloomooloo became a shanty town. The open paddocks and large estates were replaced with small, cramped houses made of cheap timber or canvas, homes for the people who worked on the harbour or in the factories that were popping up all along the foreshore.

People up on the cliffs, where Victoria Street is now, built bigger houses and good roads because they were the factory owners and the wealthy classes and had more money than the workers down in the Loo.

When the plague came in 1904, the government had to burn or destroy most of the shanty houses in the Loo because they were so flimsy and crowded. Disease spread amongst the people because they had no bathrooms or running water or anything. New houses were built. They were still cheap and crowded but not as bad as they were before.

Mrs Fowler said that the plague didn't really get up the

cliff to Victoria Street and that is why there are still so many houses here that were built before the 1900s. In fact, Victoria Street stayed posh until the end of the 1910s, but eventually the rich people up here got sick of living so close to all those poor people and so they moved further out into the eastern suburbs. That's when the big houses were turned into flats and boarding houses and filled up with migrants and casual workers and people who were coming into the city from the country areas.

That's the Victoria Street Mrs Fowler grew up in. She was born in 1912 and when she was a little girl there were no rich people left in Victoria Street, just lots of families, migrants and artists, same as it is now, really.

I wanted to ask Mrs Fowler about what it was like when she was my age and if there were any famous people who lived here then, but she was tired. She did say we could come back tomorrow afternoon and she would tell us all about Victoria Street and what it was like when she was a kid.

I reckon our history report is going to be included in the letter to the heritage people for sure!

25 FEBRUARY 1973

To hear Mrs Fowler tell it, the whole of Darlinghurst has always been one of the most exciting and famous places in Sydney. She told us about the razor gangs and a woman named Tilly Devine who ran criminal gangs all up and down the Loo, Darlinghurst and Kings Cross. Tilly was so powerful she was known as the 'Queen of Woolloomooloo'. She had an archenemy, another woman called Kate Leigh, who ran all the criminal activities over in Surry Hills, which is just across the other side of Oxford Street.

Mrs Fowler said that even though Tilly Devine ran all of the businesses, she didn't often leave her home in Palmer Street in the Loo, leaving her empire to be run by smaller gang leaders she controlled. A man named Guido Calletti ran the gangs that worked throughout Victoria Street. His gang was called the Darlinghurst Push and they were all factory workers or migrants turned standover men and criminals. Like most of the gangs that Tilly ran, they used men's shaving razors as their main weapons when fighting and brawling, so they became known as one of Sydney's razor gangs. Mrs Fowler says the place was pretty rough back then, even worse than it is now, with Tilly and Kate constantly fighting over territory.

When she was talking about the Darlinghurst Push, I couldn't help thinking about all the goons who were wandering around our street, acting all tough and making people afraid. But Mrs Fowler said the old razor gangs never deliberately hurt innocent people, just mostly fought amongst themselves for power and money.

I did think it was cool that so many women were part of Darlinghurst's history, even if some of them weren't so nice, like Tilly Devine, and I wanted to know who our street was named after. Was there another important Australian woman, maybe a wife of a governor or a famous writer or someone named Victoria who inspired the naming of our street?

There wasn't. Our street was named after a queen! Not our current queen, but one named Queen Victoria who lived way back before the turn of the twentieth century. Lots of things in Australia are named after her, including a state, a desert and a style of house. Mrs Fowler showed me a picture of Queen Victoria in a book. She looked really old, not like our current Queen Elizabeth who is young and pretty.

So, it was a rough old start for Victoria Street, but things changed for the better here after the Second World War. More migrants moved in and then the Americans came, too, and set up the naval base down on Wylde Street.

After that, Darlinghurst and Kings Cross became known as the nightclub capital of Sydney, with dance halls and nightclubs springing up everywhere.

I knew that the 1950s was when my ma came to Australia, so Susie and I decided to go and ask her about what it was like back then.

Ma was a bit shy to talk about her arrival here. She just said she came over on a big ship that took weeks to reach us. When she arrived, she couldn't speak any English, but she was quick and clever and soon she was speaking better English than people who had lived here their whole lives.

She told us that my pa was here long before she arrived. He had come over as a boy with his parents after the First World War. He lived all over Australia because his father took jobs working in factories and in cane fields and even as a jackaroo out on the stations in central Australia. But it wasn't until Pa moved into Darlinghurst in 1957 that he met my ma in one of the nightclubs up on Darlinghurst Road. Ma said back then people from all over Sydney would come into the Cross on a weekend to dance and socialise and have fun.

After Ma and Pa got married, they moved into the basement flat in Victoria Street because the rent was very cheap and neither of them had a lot of money.

Ma calls that time the 'swinging' sixties. She said it was when the Victoria Street I know really started because it was discovered by artists, writers and young families who lived right alongside sailors and factory workers and nightclub dancers. Ma says that once she moved into number 85, she finally found her home, the first one she'd had since leaving Ukraine when she was a teenager.

Listening to Ma talking about her early life here with my Pa and all the cool people she knew when she was younger, I could see how much she loved this place and how sad she would be if she ever had to leave it. Sadder than me, even.

5 MARCH 1973

Susie and I got an A+++ for our assignment on Victoria Street, which is the highest mark I have ever got for anything.

Mrs Frater said she learned a lot from reading it and it was definitely going to be included in the submission to the heritage people.

I am so happy. I mean, how often does a kid get their thoughts listened to by important people like that!

8 MARCH 1973

Today I had a blue with Tommo Jenkins!

Ma sent me and Darren off to Mr Botticelli's store to get some eggs and OJ so we would have something for breakfast tomorrow. I had to take Darren along because Ma was trying to get ready for work. He never likes me to go anywhere without him anyhow.

Problem is, when I go to the shops, I have to leave Darren waiting outside. He's likely to knock over things or open packets of sweets and eat them—even though he knows we don't have the money to pay for them! Darren doesn't mean to do the wrong thing; he just doesn't understand. But Mr Botticelli is a bit of an old grump, so if he catches Darren doing it again, he might ban us from the shop for good.

I think Mr Botticelli hates kids in general, but I think he hates us Vic Street kids in particular because he is always yelling at us and accusing us of nicking stuff, which we almost never do. So, I sat Darren on the little walled fence on the corner of Challis Avenue and told him to wait for me.

I bought all the stuff on Ma's list—bread, four eggs and

a bottle of orange juice—and spent the cent left over on a peppermint humbug for Darren. I had to balance it all in my arms because I forgot to bring a carry bag, even though Ma reminded me.

As I came out of the store, I saw Tommo Jenkins standing over Darren. Leaning into him, all menacing-like. Now, I am not one to start a fight. And I'm not very big or very strong. But I had to get my brother away from Tommo. I could hear Tommo teasing Darren, who doesn't understand that Tommo is a threat. Darren is the kind of kid who wants to be mates with everyone. That's not a good way to deal with Tommo Jenkins, though, and Darren grinning up at him and being nice was just making Tommo meaner and meaner.

Even as far away as I was, I could hear it in Tommo's voice. He was mad because Darren wasn't acting scared like he was supposed to. Suddenly, Tommo had Darren by the shoulders and began to shake him, asking him if he was an idiot.

I got madder than anything seeing my brother being treated like that. I didn't even care that it was Tommo Jenkins—three years older than me and fifty times as mean. I just flew towards him, pegging the bottle of orange juice right at his face.

I don't have a great throw, so it landed a bit short,

but the explosion as the glass bottle hit the pavement and then splattered up all over his pants scared Tommo nearly to death. I swear he jumped right out of his skin and ran off like a rat up a drainpipe.

I don't think he knew what was happening. He probably thought it was gunfire, or he'd been attacked by a ninja or an ogre or something. He just took off like a coward, right down Challis Avenue towards Darlo Road.

I could have left it at that and I know I should have. But I was still so mad. So, I started pegging the eggs at him, too, and one of them hit him right in the back of the head. Bullseye!

He stopped then and looked back at me. And he sees I'm not a ninja or an ogre. I'm just a smaller-than-average eleven-year-old girl with an arm full of groceries. His expression changed and he was running back towards me, roaring with rage.

I grabbed Darren's hand and we ran fast as we could up Macleay Street, dodging into Orwell Lane.

Darren can't run fast, but he has stamina and Tommo's too heavy to put in much of an effort, especially when he was already puffed out from running away in the first place. He was soon panting and huffing and he gave up when I pulled Darren into Hughes Street. Darren and I didn't slow down, though.

Running up and down the McElhone Stairs to school every day keeps us both pretty fit, which is lucky for us.

Ma was so cross at me when we got home and she saw I only had the bread and not the other things she had asked me to buy. I told her I had dropped them all and they broke on the way home. I didn't want to tell her that I had thrown our food away when it was so hard for her to earn the money to pay for it.

She was still mad, though, and thanks to that mullet head, Tommo, we have nothing to eat but dry toast till Ma has enough money to buy more groceries!

Worse still, I am going to have to make sure I avoid that bully as much as I can for the next few days until he forgets about the eggs.

I hate Tommo Jenkins so much. I wish his house had been knocked down and him and his family forced to move away, but they all live up in Potts Point in a big new house his father bought with money he makes from real estate. So Tommo Jenkins is here to stay.

12 MARCH 1973

Just my luck! Today Tommo decided to come to school and I was there all on my own.

Tony the Cat was helping his father out at the fish shop. Mr Gatto is getting too old for all the heavy lifting, so he needs one of his boys to help out. The twins can't do it because they are starting at TAFE. Mr Gatto wants them to get a proper trade certificate and become plumbers.

My best mate Susie, who would usually never miss school, had a stomach flu and was staying home, probably for the next week, so I was pretty much on my own. I did my best to avoid Tommo all day, but he was giving me the hairy eyeball all through class time and he followed me out into the playground as soon as the bell rang for recess.

I'm not afraid of Tommo, but I was on my Pat Malone, so I decided to get out of his sight and read my library book behind the girls toilets. It's usually pretty safe there because the smell of the toilets mixed with the cafeteria is pretty awful.

But Tommo knew I would be there and he turned up with two of his Grade Six mates. Tommo doesn't care that I'm a girl, and he knows that without my mates I'm a sitting duck. I knew he was planning to hurt me if I didn't get away quickly, so I ran into the girls toilets and stayed there the whole recess. Even Tommo Jenkins won't go into the girls toilets.

Luckily, Mrs Garth saw Tommo and the other boys hanging around outside after the bell rang. She clipped Tommo across the ear and made him go back inside.

Even Tommo is afraid of Mrs Garth, so he did what she said. But I know he's still out to get me, so I didn't go back to class at all, just waited in the toilets all through lunchtime and right up until just before the bell rang to let Darren out of infant school. I don't know how I am going to make up the lessons I missed today, but I think Mrs Frater will give me some extra homework if I said I got sick.

I hope the Vic Street gang are back tomorrow because I don't know how long I can keep hiding from Tommo.

13 MARCH 1973

No Vic Street gang again today, so I had to spend another recess and lunchtime in the toilets. That would have been bad enough, but it was made worse because today was one of those rare days when Ma gave me lunch money instead of making sandwiches because she was running late for work. So instead of going to the canteen and getting some raisin bread, I was left sitting in a toilet cubicle, starving the whole break time.

I wasn't going to miss more class, though, because I already had a lot to catch up on as well as a spelling test in the afternoon. So, when the bell rang for end of lunch, I checked that there was no sign of Tommo in the quad or around the toilets and went back into class. Mrs Frater must have got the same flu Susie had, because she was away and the substitute teacher forgot all about our spelling test and is making us do maths problems. I hate maths so I am journaling instead.

Tommo is being awful, flicking rubber bands at me and whispering about me to his mates, and the teacher isn't doing anything.

From what I can hear, it sounds like he is going to try and get me on the way home.

There are three main staircases that we can take from Woolloomooloo up to Victoria Street, but most of us Vic Street kids use the McElhone Stairs, a big wide staircase so steep and so long it's nicknamed 'the Stairs of Death'.

There are loads of stories about tourists having heart attacks trying to make their way up from the harbour to the Cross on the Stairs of Death. I don't really believe those rumours, but Ma once told me that people did die from climbing up Mount Everest in Nepal and the McElhone Stairs had to be just as hard to climb, so maybe some of the stories are true.

There are also the Hordern Stairs, steep rickety steps that run up alongside and hug the cliffs all the way up to the top. Darren is scared of using those stairs because you feel like you are right on the edge of falling off the whole way up. So, if we didn't use the McElhone Stairs, we mainly used the Butler Stairs, which are cut into the rock of the Woolloomooloo ridge, off Broughton Street, near Rowena Place, and come up just near Mrs Fowler's flat at number 115 Victoria Street. The stone stairs are much darker than the other staircases because the stairs are narrow and bordered by sandstone rock on both sides. But that was good because it meant there was nowhere for Tommo to hide and jump out at us as we came up, like there was on the McElhone Stairs. So I decided that was our best way home. They are also farther from Tommo's house and knowing how lazy he is, I am pretty certain that if he is planning anything, it would be on the McElhone Stairs.

I hope I'm right.

14 MARCH 1973

Sorry I didn't write anything else yesterday when I got home. I completely forgot, but here is what happened.

Darren and I walked up the Butler Stairs, just like I planned we would. When we were halfway up, Darren dawdling behind me as usual, a lumbering man came stumbling down the steps and completely blocked our way. He wasn't a big man and, at first, I was sure it was Tommo, waiting for me on the Butler Stairs after all.

But it wasn't Tommo. It was my pa. I knew as soon as he called my name. My full name, Wilomena.

Only my dad has ever called me Wilomena. I was surprised he even remembered my name; I mean, we haven't spoken to him in years, not since he left us back when Darren was only a baby. Yet there he was, standing there using my name like he had every right to.

He was wearing a big pea-green duffle coat and his face was covered in a coarse, greying beard, which is why I didn't recognise him at first.

I asked him what he wanted, but instead of answering he just grinned at me. He had horrible crooked yellow teeth and as he came nearer, I smelled how badly he reeked from sweat and lack of washing. He held a bottle in his left hand, a quarter full with some brown liquid, and a crinkled-up newspaper in his right hand. I was ready to run, thinking he was going to try and grab me. He didn't, though. Just shuffled back and forth saying that stupid name he gave me, over and over again.

'Wilomena, Wilomena.'

I told him my name was Billie, not Wilomena, but he ignored me like always. 'Wilomena,' he replied, 'Do ya have any money you could give your old pa?'

I told him I didn't and he called me a liar and some other words which I won't write down here. I thought he knew I had the lunch money Ma gave me, though I don't know how he could have known.

It didn't matter. I wasn't going to give him any of it. I just pushed past him, dragging Darren behind me. As we passed, he spat right at Darren and the spit landed on my brother's shirt. It was disgusting and green and I wiped it off right away with the sleeve of my own dress. Pa has always been particularly mean to Darren and it makes me really mad because Darren has never done anything to deserve it. All he ever wants is to make everyone happy and never does a mean thing to anyone. So I yelled at my pa and told him to get lost!

I know it's a bad thing to talk disrespectfully to your pa and I am sorry that I did it, but only because it frightened Darren even more and he started to cry. Pa smirked at that, like he was happy that my little brother was crying. Which made me madder still.

I hugged my brother and told him we were better off without our father, loud enough for Pa to hear, but instead of getting mad, Pa turned his back on us and picked up a discarded cigarette butt someone had tossed on the ground.

I was still mad, but I didn't curse at him again, I swear, I just took Darren's hand and walked away, trying to cheer up my brother and stop him from crying.

Pa didn't try to follow us and I thought he had forgotten all about us until I was at the top of the stairs and he called out again. He was sitting on the steps by then, his back pressed up against the wall. He wasn't even looking at us as he said, 'You should help out your old pa, Wilomena, you owe me.'

I didn't know what to say. I didn't owe him anything. He was the one who had walked out on us. Left Ma and me and Darren with nothing, just ran off with a woman from up on Macleay Street. It wasn't my fault she worked out he wasn't worth her time and threw him out. He owed me. He owed me a father who would look out for us, a father who worked and paid the bills and made sure my ma and Darren and me were safe from all the bad things in the world. I don't owe him a thing.

But I knew better than to say any of that. What difference would it make anyway? My pa was no good and that wasn't going to change. So I just led Darren up the stairs and out into Victoria Street, telling him not to say anything to Ma about seeing Pa.

I don't know why, but I think seeing my Pa on the steps yesterday was a really, really bad omen.

17 MARCH 1973

Susie has been sick all week and I have been dying to see her. Ma had forbidden me to even visit or check on her until word comes that Susie isn't throwing up anymore.

'Last thing I need is you catching whatever Susie has and being off sick for a week, too!' was what Ma said. I wouldn't mind getting sick and having two weeks off and having Ma making me soup like Susie's mum does.

This morning Susie's mum called in to say I can finally visit. I can even come around today and watch *Young Talent Time* with them if I want to.

Of course, I do! I miss Susie desperately and I miss watching TV almost as much.

Susie is the only person I know who has a television set. Well, the TV actually belongs to Susie's sister Sherry, who is sixteen and works part-time as a hairdressing assistant, which is why she can afford something as expensive as a television set. Sherry bought it second-hand and it only gets two channels—and only in blurry black and white—but watching it with Susie is my favourite thing to do ever.

Ma said I can go, as long as I help with the washing and folding and have my bath before I leave, but I wasn't quick enough and now I am writing this while I wait for the Finnegan kids to get out of the bathroom. One of those kids always seems to be in the bath or the downstairs dunny, especially if I desperately need to use it.

And when they do finally get out of the bathroom, the room is always soaking wet and the water in the tub is brown with filth.

Don't tell Ma, but I plan to pull the plug and have fresh water from the tap once the Finnegans are out. We aren't supposed to refill the bath every time, so usually I try to be first in the tub, but today I was just too slow.

Don't get me wrong, I don't mind sharing my bath water with Darren or Ma, but there is no way I am hopping into old Finnegan water!

It's almost half past five now and *Young Talent Time* starts at 6 pm on the dot. I don't want to be late.

I wish those kids would stop screaming and splashing about and get out of the bathroom already. I won't have time to do a proper wash now. Maybe I can skip the bath. I mean, how much dirt can be on me.

I think I am just going to go. I can always have an extra scrub next week if potatoes really do start to grow behind my ears as Ma always says they will.

LATER

It was so good to see Susie tonight, but the evening didn't work out exactly as I expected.

Susie is my best friend in the whole wide world. We are almost the exact same age, born on the same day but in different months in 1962. But she doesn't look anything like me. Susie is small and olive skinned like the rest of her family, with short glossy black hair that never goes frizzy. She has brown eyes and big thick eyebrows that make her look like she is always thinking hard.

She lives in the flat at the back of number 93, which is a few doors down the street from us. Her house is bigger than ours, with three stories split into six two-room flats. Their only dunny is out the back in the garden, so anyone who needs to use it has to walk past Susie's window. We always used to call out to them as they were going by and say we were timing them. They told Susie's mum and now there's a big red curtain across the window to stop us looking out.

I like Susie's flat better than our rooms. Hers is like a proper flat, with two rooms, one of which used to be the kitchen of the house before it was broken up into all the different flats. It even has an old stove that still works, so Susie's mum can cook proper food and not just stuff on an old hotplate like the rest of the flats have to use. Susie's mum and dad sleep next to the stove on a big red couch that folds out into a bed and folds back up when everyone wants to sit on it to watch the telly. The other, smaller room is for Sherry, Susie and Angelica to sleep in. But because Sherry is out so much with her boyfriend, and Anjelica is just a tiny baby, it often feels like Susie has a whole bedroom all to herself. I'm almost as jealous of that as I am of Sherry's TV!

I like Susie's family, especially Angelica, who is a very sweet and quiet baby. I'm not so keen on Sherry, though, because she can be a bit mean—especially about her television.

She was grumpier than usual tonight, because their mum said Susie and I could watch the telly sitting on Susie's bed, rather than on the couch in the big room. Sherry complained because that meant she had to drag the telly into the bedroom and set it all up again. Sherry hates moving the telly if she doesn't have to because the picture drops out when you move the antenna and it can take ages to fiddle around to get it back. I tried to help her by clearing some of her makeup and hairbrushes and stuff from the top of the chest of drawers, but she acted like I was just getting in the way. So I decided to leave her to it and jumped up on the bed beside Susie instead.

Susie was sitting up on her mattress, looking a bit pale, but grinning from ear to ear, so I knew she must be feeling better.

I had missed her so much while she was sick and was so glad to see her that I flung my arms around her and hugged her tight. Susie said I couldn't squeeze her so much because she might still throw up, so I moved back a bit, just to be on the safe side.

Sherry took ages messing around with the rabbit-ear antenna on the telly, trying to get the fuzzy grey and black dots to form into some kind of picture. Finally it cleared and we could see the round, happy faces of the Talent Time cast singing the latest pop hit. Sherry stood back and turned the volume knob up loudly so the room was filled with the voices of the teenage stars singing 'Sunshine, Lollipops'. Sometimes she's all right, really.

I jumped off the bed, grabbed Sherry's tortoiseshell hairbrush and began dancing and singing along like I was one of the YTT kids. I reckon I would be aces on that show if they ever came and asked me to be part of the team. Maybe I can't sing all that well, but what I lack in talent I make up for in volume!

Susie was rolling about laughing, but Sherry didn't look impressed and snatched her brush off me and flounced out of the room.

I knew she wouldn't be gone for long, though.

Sherry always insisted on changing the channel to Bandstand halfway through our show because she had to watch all the older kids dancing and the bands playing live and she said YTT was for babies. It is not! But I don't mind watching Bandstand because sometimes they have Sherbet on and I think Daryl Braithwaite is the most handsome man in the whole world.

But before Sherry had even closed the door on us, I heard the sound of smashing glass coming from the front of the house, followed by a louder, violent crashing sound. Susie and I hesitated for a moment, but when we heard Susie's parents going out into the hallway, we both jumped up and went out to see what was happening.

It was crazy what we saw. Mr and Mrs Angelov were already out of the flat and in the main hallway, looking at the front door of the house, which had been battered in. Anjelica was cradled in Mrs Angelov's arms and she seemed as quiet and shocked as the rest of us, even though she was less than a year old. The window above the door handle had been smashed and the glass glistened like glitter on the swirly pink carpeted entryway.

There were three bricks lying on the floor. Even from where I was standing, I could see that words had been scrawled across the bricks in black permanent marker.

Mrs Angelov ushered us all back into the flat and closed the door while Susie's dad stayed in the hallway picking up the bricks and the larger shards of glass.

As we returned to the flat, Sherry said it was the third time this week something like this had happened and that was why the other tenants were all moving out. I realised then how no other tenants had come out of their flats to see what was going on.

'We should be leaving, too,' Sherry said. 'Those men won't stop harassing us until we do.'

Her mum gave Sherry a hard look and then told us that it wasn't anything to worry about and it would probably all blow over in a few days.

Susie and I went back into the bedroom, but both of us were a bit shaken up and we barely paid any attention to the end of the show. Sherry didn't come in and change the channel and we got to watch the whole episode all the way through to the end. But all I could think about was the words I had seen scrawled across the brick that someone had thrown through the window.

GET OUT NOW, that's what it had said.

18 MARCH 1973

Susie told me she doesn't know why men are throwing bricks through her window and her parents refused to answer any of my questions when I asked them. They both seemed very upset, though, and Mr Angelov insisted on walking me all the way back to my house after *Young Talent Time*, even though daylight savings hasn't ended yet and it was still light at 8.30 pm. He didn't talk to me the whole walk home. He seemed worried, constantly looking over his shoulder as we walked down past the few houses that separated my house from his. I noticed a lot of them were empty.

Mr Angelov didn't say anything to Ma when he dropped me off, just nodded and bid her good evening and then walked back. But Ma could tell something wasn't right, so I told her what had happened at Susie's and how all the other residents in their flats had moved out. She didn't say anything, but she didn't look shocked or surprised.

I asked why someone would throw a brick through Susie's front door and at first Ma didn't want to say too much, but finally she sat down and told me that there have been things like that happening on the street for a while.

'Mr Carson, the man who owns the houses, wants everyone to move out because he wants to replace all the houses with a carpark,' she said. 'But people are refusing to move and so the landlord is getting a bit nasty.'

Ma also told me that Susie's parents had been told to move over a week ago, but they, too, were refusing to go. 'They don't have to leave because they have a lease and that means they can stay until it runs out in October. But Mr Carson wants everyone out before that.'

'Do we have a lease?' I asked. Ma said we did and that we paid our rent and Carson wasn't allowed by law to make anyone leave who didn't want to.

I told her I didn't want to leave and she asked why.

'Because this is my home,' I said. 'And people should be able to stay in their homes.'

My ma said that was exactly how she felt and that we were not leaving and neither were Susie and her family.

'You don't give into bullies,' she said. And I agree with her. Bullies are the worst thing ever.

2 APRIL 1973

I had a terrible nightmare last night. I dreamed that I woke up and there were bulldozers coming through our walls and burying me and Ma and Darren under a pile of rubble.

I know it's just a dream, but it's true in a way, too, because those bulldozers down in the Loo just keep coming at the people standing and lying in front of them, yelling and singing.

So far, the bulldozers haven't rolled over anyone, but if they did, I bet they wouldn't even care. And once they have knocked down all the houses in the Loo, then they will come up here and Mr Carson will use them to clear all our houses and build his carpark. Would he care if we were all underneath it, even as he built right over the top of us?

I don't think he would.

5 APRIL 1973

Mrs Frater gave me an A+ for my spelling worksheet today. She says I am doing very well, so it would have been a great day except that Tommo Jenkins turned up for the first time in a week and as soon as he saw me, he decided to come and have a blue in the school hallway. He thought better of it when he realised all the Vic Street gang were back, though. Tommo Jenkins might be a bully, but he was outnumbered.

Mrs Garth was checking the hallway making sure we all went out into the quad because the building is off limits in break times. We all hurried out before she could give us detention, but Tommo wasn't fast enough and she gave him a real ear bashing—not just for being in the corridor but also for missing detention last week.

Mrs Garth is always yelling at Tommo about something. I don't like Tommo, but I don't think Mrs Garth needs to be so mean, either. Maybe that's where Tommo gets it from?

10 APRIL 1973

Great news! The bulldozers down in Woolloomooloo have stopped!

Everyone at school was talking about it—how the men driving the machines just walked away and no-one turned up to drive them the next day.

It's all because a group called the BLF, which stands for the Builders' Labourers' Federation, did a green ban, which means they said that no-one who works for the Federation will demolish or help to build anything down in the Loo until the residents are properly listened to and the houses are kept intact.

The BLF did the same thing in loads of other places like Centennial Park and The Rocks and the bulldozers and wrecking balls had to go away. I think it's amazing.

There's still a big old empty construction site right in the middle of the Loo, though, with half-demolished buildings and debris everywhere. The bulldozers could come back, but Mrs Frater says that the people in the Loo are safe for now.

I found out that the BLF is also going to put a green ban on Victoria Street, even before any bulldozers come in! I am really happy about this because I have had that same horrible bulldozer nightmare three nights in a row this week. Now it looks like I really don't need to worry.

With the BLF looking after us, I reckon those mean bullies throwing bricks through windows and calling us nasty names on the street will have to back off. And Susie and her family will be safe.

I think being a builder's labourer sounds cool. That's what I am going to be when I grow up now, instead of a nurse. I saw there were women who were builder's labourers, too, so I can definitely be one if I want to. I never liked the idea of being a nurse anyway because I don't really like the sight of blood.

20 APRIL 1973

It's Good Friday and the Vic gang are spending all day today blowing the insides out of the rotten eggs from Kim Hannigan's chook pens.

It smells rank, but it will all be worth it when we paint the eggs with our textas.

I'm going to decorate mine with polka dots.

22 APRIL 1973

I love Easter.

Mrs Gatto cooked us hot cross buns which we had with melted butter, and Rev Ted at Wayside Chapel hosted a big Easter egg competition.

My polka dot eggs won best design in the contest and I got a huge chocolate egg wrapped in shiny green foil as a prize. I gave half of it to Darren. He ate it all in one go and it made him feel really sick. But he was enjoying it so much it felt mean to tell him to stop eating it.

I'm saving mine, though. I'm only going to eat a tiny bit each day and that way it will last me almost till Christmas!

We're off on the Easter egg hunt now. I already know where all the eggs are because I helped Ma put them along the street, but it's fun to help Darren find them. I'm a bit too old for the hunt now.

25 APRIL 1973

It's Anzac Day and we all went to the Domain at dawn to see the parade and wave to Mr Stanislav who lives down the street and marches with the Second World War soldiers every year. I hate having to get up so early, but Ma insists. She says we have to respect the soldiers who fought for us.

My ma was in Europe during the last big war. Not the one going on now, which is in South-East Asia, but the one before that—which was in Europe and was started by people called the Nazis who lived in Germany.

My pa is German and as much as I don't like him, he was never as bad as a Nazi. He hated the Nazis as much as Ma did. He was already in Australia long before the Second World War started, but because of the Nazis he and his family were put in a place that's called an internment camp, just because he was German. Even though he had been living here since he was younger than me! German and Japanese people who lived in Australia at that time were all put in these camps because the government worried they might be spies and tell their governments back in Japan and Germany what Australians were doing. I think that sounds a bit unfair. People can't help where they are born. What's really funny is Ma says that my pa didn't even speak German before he went into the camp. He learned it while he was being held with all those other Australian-Germans and came out of there with a really strong German accent.

I don't think my Pa wanted to be here in Victoria Street, or even in Australia, but my ma, like me, doesn't ever want to be anywhere else.

27 APRIL 1973

Everything has been just awful today! Susie told me that even though the bulldozers have stopped, the thugs are still hassling her and her family. They are the only ones left in their building now and Susie reckons her mum is already talking about leaving.

I can't imagine life without my best friend and I am so angry and sad. I have been in a bad mood all day.

To cheer me up, Tony suggested we all go down to the abandoned building site in the Loo on our way home from school to look for treasure. I knew I wasn't supposed to go anywhere near the building sites. Ma is worried we could tread on a rusty nail or get crushed by one of the still standing walls and she made me promise not to go or to let Darren go.

But that was weeks ago and nothing has happened to any of the other kids who go there all the time. So, I reckoned it couldn't be that dangerous really.

And there was sure to be treasure hidden under the mounds of rubble, so I let Tony talk me into it and I made Darren promise not to dob us in to Ma so he could come, too.

It was really easy getting in. There were so many holes in the cheap fencing and we could see where other kids had gone in and explored before us. Going there did cheer me up a lot, even though it was hard to look for treasure while watching Darren. All he wanted to do was play on the bulldozer which was just abandoned there in the middle of the site. We couldn't start it up or anything, but Darren was happy to hang off it like a monkey bar or pretend to drive it around, so that was okay.

My awful day was actually turning out to be quite good. Susie and Tony were finding some treasure and I was having fun playing bulldozers with my brother. The sun was shining and all our cares seemed really far away.

But then Tommo Jenkins turned up.

I saw him skulking about behind what was left of the walls, the ones that had **SAVE THE LOO** and **SUPPORT THE BLF** written on them. I wasn't even sure I had seen him at first, it was so shadowy. But then he started walking towards Susie, who was all on her own on the far side of the site.

Tommo wasn't on his own, though. Two of his high school mates were trailing after him like loyal, ugly dogs.

I yelled to Susie and she looked up and saw them, but it was too late. They had her backed up against one of the fences without any gaps in it. Tony the Cat was way over on the other side and even though I know he's quick, I didn't think he would be able to reach Susie as fast as I could. So it was up to me to try to protect her.

I told Darren to stay by the bulldozer and ran over to the bullies and pushed past them through to Susie, telling Tommo and his mates to rack off. Tommo just laughed at me.

'You gonna fight all of us, Billie Boy's Name?' he asked.

I hate how he called me that stupid nickname. Billie isn't a boy's name! It's my name and I am a girl. So it's obviously a girl's name! He's so stupid.

Anyway, I told him to go away, but he knew we were there hunting for treasure because that was what he was doing, too. He made Susie open her clenched fist and show him what she had collected.

She had a whole fistful of coins. Most of them were useless—old money like shillings and a few farthings that you couldn't use, except sometimes in the arcade machines and phone boxes which could be tricked to think they were the new money. But she also had a few proper coins, a five and two ten cent pieces.

My heart sank when I saw Tommo grab them out of Susie's hand and put them in his pocket.

It's bad enough that he stole Susie's treasure but then, just to be mean, he pushed her backwards into the dirt.

I hate Tommo Jenkins. Always picking on me and Susie because he thinks we're just weak girls who can't fight back.

I can though and I showed him so, clawing his face with my hands as he stumbled backwards.

He wasn't expecting it and a few of my swipes tore at his cheeks, leaving ugly red welts. I heard Darren running up behind me and yelled at him to run home to Victoria Street because I didn't want him to get hurt.

I knew I wasn't going to win a fight against Tommo Jenkins and I had been mad to even try! The three of those big boys against the three of us fifth graders wasn't a fair fight and Tommo knew it. We were in for it for sure!

That's when we heard a big burly voice boom from somewhere across the building site.

'What are youse ratbags doing here?'

All of us froze and looked over to the road where a huge man in a blue work shirt was striding towards us, a look of fury on his face. We looked at each other and then, without a word, all ran off in different directions, scattering like flies off a garbage bin.

I saw Tommo and one of his mates duck behind a huge mound of dirt at the edge of the site. But us Vic Street kids ran for the hole in the fence and then down the road towards the church on McElhone Street which was a local shortcut to Broughton Street and the Butler Stairs. Darren was hiding behind the church waiting for me. I hugged him quickly and then we were all running up the Butler Stairs, puffing and panting, away from the concrete and asphalt wasteland of Woolloomooloo, into Victoria Street and safety.

By the time we got home, Darren was crying and Ma knew something was up. I know he didn't mean to dob on me, but I'm grounded for the whole weekend now!

I don't think my life could get any worse!

30 APRIL 1973

Today Mrs Fowler wasn't sitting at her window like she usually is when we pass by her on our way home from school. Instead, she was sitting out in the middle of the street in a plastic lawn chair.

I knew something wasn't right straight away because Mrs Fowler hardly ever comes outside, but when she does, she always makes sure she looks her best, with her hair done and her lipstick on, wearing her best winter coat and her dead fox scarf slung around her neck.

But there she was sitting outside in her nightdress in the middle of the afternoon. She didn't have any shoes on and only a thin blanket around her shoulders to protect her from the cold.

Susie and Darren and I ran up to her and asked her if she was okay. But she didn't seem to know who we were, she was so upset.

'It's me, Billie from down the street, number 85. And this is Susie. You know us, Mrs Fowler. What's happened? Why are you sitting out here?' I saw that all of Mrs Fowler's possessions were piled up on the street around her.

Mrs Fowler's son Mick was nowhere to be seen. And you can't miss Mick Fowler if he is around. He is a huge, bruising bloke, always dressed in navy work shirts, thick roped jumpers, jeans and heavy black hobnail boots. His face is weathered from the ocean and he has a pug-like look about him that makes everyone immediately take him seriously. He is often away for weeks and months at a time working on the boats that travel to the US or England while Mrs Fowler just waits in the flat for him to come home.

But today Mrs Fowler didn't seem to know what was going on; we couldn't get any sense out of her at all.

I didn't understand what was happening either, until a muscly blond man with a handlebar moustache, carrying a pickaxe handle, walked out of Mrs Fowler's building. He was ordering some other blokes to board up the windows and nail big **NO ENTRY** signs on the door.

Susie went pale when she saw him and whispered that he was the man who was coming around to their house all the time making threats and telling her parents they had to move out or he would have them thrown out.

I wondered if that was what was happening to Mrs Fowler. Why were these men throwing her out of her home, tossing her out on the street along with all her things?

I knew a lot of the other residents of 115 had left already because I had seen them packing their cars and moving out weeks before. But Mrs Fowler told everyone who would listen that she wasn't moving—no matter what.

But here she was, with no-one to protect her or look out for her. And these thugs didn't care that Mrs Fowler didn't want to leave. That she had to be there when her son came home from sea.

When the coppers arrived, I thought they would march right up to those thugs and sort them right out. But they didn't. Instead, they walked up to us and told Mrs Fowler that she was breaking the law by loitering there and leaving the street littered with all her stuff. Then they told her to pick up her rubbish and move along!

I couldn't believe what I was hearing. I mean, the coppers didn't do much for us here on Victoria Street at the best of times, but couldn't they see that Mrs Fowler was the victim?

Someone had to stand up for her and there was only me and my friends to do it.

'It's those blokes you should be moving on!' I said to the coppers, pointing at the man with the pickaxe handle and his mates. The cops ignored me because I'm just a kid and cops never listen to kids, especially not Vic Street ones.

Behind us, the muscle men continued to board up the windows and the coppers did nothing.

'They threw me out!' Mrs Fowler tried to tell the policeman, 'with nothing but this!' She opened her fist to reveal a fifty-dollar bill crumpled in her palm.

The older policeman, a sergeant he was, just looked at the money and shrugged. 'This looks like a legal eviction then, ma'am,' the Sergeant said. 'They've even given you compensation like they have to by law. You need to move on now.'

I was going to start yelling at the coppers there and then.

How could they be so mean and unfair? Mrs Fowler hadn't done anything wrong. But before I could work out exactly what to say, a woman dressed in black jeans and a skivvy turned up from nowhere and started yelling at the cops. She was the same woman who was often out rallying on the street and asking everyone to come along to the resident meetings. The thugs called her names and threw rubbish and beer at her when she was speaking, but it didn't stop her, so I knew she was fearless. But today I realised she was totally awesome. And she yelled at the thugs as well. The cops told her to calm down or they would arrest her, but she just stuck her tongue out at the sergeant and then came over and asked us if we were all right and if we needed any help. She told us her name was Lucy and that she and a lot of other people were squatting in some of the abandoned houses on Victoria Street. She said Mrs Fowler could come and stay with them if she needed to, but Mrs Fowler didn't want to go anywhere with a stranger, so I said she could come and stay with us until Mick came back. Lucy thought that was a good idea and told me it was important that we keep as many people in our house as we could because as long as people were in the house, even if there had been eviction orders, the landlord wasn't allowed to knock it down. He would have to wait for the heritage people to make the decision about the houses like he promised he would.

I really wanted to talk to her more about what all that meant and what else we could do to stop the evil landlord, but it was starting to rain and Mrs Fowler was so cold and frail looking that I thought I'd better get her back to our place so she could warm up and wait for Ma to come home and help her decide what to do next.

Lucy said that she would get some of her mates to come and pick up Mrs Fowler's things and put them somewhere safe, which was really nice of her. She also said that if we needed any other help, we could find her or one of her mates living at number 112.

Mrs Fowler is downstairs with Ma in our kitchen now. I don't know what she is going to do. I don't think she knows either.

2 MAY 1973

Mrs Fowler is staying in the back room of our house now because Mr Lionel moved out a few days ago.

He said he didn't like how rough the street was getting and he could write his books from anywhere. He's the first of the people in our house to move out. I hope no-one else goes.

Ma said I did the right thing bringing Mrs Fowler here and when Mick comes home everything will be sorted out. Mrs Fowler says he's due back any day now. I hope he comes quick. It's nice having Mrs Fowler here, but she wants to be in her own house and I don't blame her.

I told Ma about Lucy and how she talked about fighting back against the thugs and bullies who tossed out Mick's mum. Then I told her how Susie reckons he's the same thug who is picking on her family. Ma didn't say anything, but she looked really worried.

Later I heard her tell Mrs Gatto that Lucy was probably a communist and she didn't want me or Darren getting mixed up with people like that.

5 MAY 1973

Mick Fowler has just turned up on our doorstep looking grim and determined, asking if his mum is here.

Ma has taken him into the kitchen and they are all drinking tea and talking in hushed voices so I have to pretend to be busy writing in this book so they won't notice me and tell me to go to our room.

I can hear them pretty well from where I am sitting on the bottom of the staircase. Mum is telling Mick what happened and she even mentioned me and how nice I was to help Mrs Fowler and bring her here.

Mick says I am a brave girl and he was glad I was there. My heart is swelling with pride. Mick Fowler doesn't say much to anyone, but he's someone everyone on this street respects.

I can only imagine what sort of trouble he is planning against those who messed with his mum! All the time my ma and Mick were talking, I could see a load of other men standing around outside our door. They all look a lot like Mick—big and strong, wearing navy pants and thick, heavy sweaters. I reckon they must be Mick's mates from down the docks and off the ships. Sailors and dock workers and fisherman here to help Mick take his flat back.

I feel sorry for those thugs if these blokes have a blue with them. Oh, Mick is leaving.

They are heading off down the street now. I am going to follow them. I'll write all about it when I get back …

LATER!

Ma caught me and Darren trying to follow the men down the street and told us we had to stay inside. But then Mrs Fowler wanted to go and one of Mick's mates promised to look out for us and I think Ma wanted to see what was going to happen too, so we all walked down to number 115 together, although Ma made us promise to stay right out of any shenanigans.

By the time we got to Mick's flat, all the men were already there, but we were in time to see the real action and it was the stuff of legend. And I was right there, right as it was happening.

Pickaxe and his thugs weren't expecting any real trouble, so when Mick and the rest of them marched up that street, I don't reckon they knew what was going on. As Mick's men poured into the front garden, the blokes inside just stared through the windows, not knowing what to do.

Mick walked up to the front door and knocked on it, all calm, and the man with the pickaxe handle opened the door and stepped out, all blustering, his chest puffed out in his fluro green T-shirt. But Mick just stays calm and says, 'Mate, this is my house. What are you doing?'

Pickaxe stood there, his legs apart, holding the long handle of the axe across his day-glo chest, making him look like a sentry in an old movie.

'This isn't your house, mate. This is the property of Mr Carson,' Pickaxe said.

'Look, I'm Mick Fowler,' Mick says. 'I'm the legal tenant, I live here. My gear's been put out, my mother has been thrown on the street and the joint's been broken into. I'm very upset. I've just come back from sea to find this and it's not on. All right, just leave now and there won't be any trouble.'

Pickaxe looked out past Mick and saw all the seamen and dock workers standing in the yard and around the street. Other neighbours had come out of their houses as well, thinking something big might be about to happen. Even someone as dumb as Pickaxe must have known he was completely outnumbered.

But that man was dumber than he looked.

'Can't do that, mate,' Pickaxe said, instead of backing down. 'I'm here legally, your mother took the money and left of her own choice. Nothing you can do about it. If you don't leave, I'll call the cops on you.'

Mick nodded and stepped away.

I thought maybe he had given up. Pickaxe obviously had the same thought because he smirked and relaxed a bit, his axe handle dropping slightly. He definitely thought the confrontation was over.

He was wrong.

Mick gave a little wave and all his men surged forwards, revealing crowbars, screwdrivers and hammers. Pickaxe, looking alarmed, ran back inside, slamming and locking the door behind him. It didn't matter. The men ripped off the boards like they were paper and were soon bashing through the front door.

Mrs Fowler, Ma, me and Darren stood back watching in awe as three big burly goons were picked up like feathers by a gang of seamen and hoisted out of the house and onto the street.

Mick had Pickaxe by the scruff of his neck and ran him all the way down the front path, throwing him in a heap on the road.

Pickaxe spluttered and cursed, but there was nothing he could do. His mates all ran away and more of Mick's men arrived, along with Lucy and a few of her mates, carrying Mrs Fowler's rescued possessions back into that house so Pickaxe couldn't do anything.

Then Mick picked up his old mum and carried her inside as all of us cheered them on.

And Mrs Fowler even got to keep that fifty dollars they gave her.

15 MAY 1973

It's been two weeks since Mick threw those thugs out of his flat and things on the street have calmed down a bit. Susie even reckons they have backed off her house and it looks like they may stay in the street after all.

I'm so glad! I was really worried that her parents would make Susie move somewhere far away. The other residents who have been leaving talked about going as far as the Central Coast or places I have never heard of like Mount Druitt and Rooty Hill.

3 JUNE 1973

Tony the Cat got his pay for working with his dad today and he was really cool and offered to buy us all Sunnyboys from Mr Botticelli's shop. I reckon Tony the Cat has a little crush on Susie and that's why he offered. I don't mind, though. Tony is a pretty cool guy and I think Susie should start going out with him, but Susie only has eyes for Jacko, who never pays her any attention.

Of course, as soon as we entered the shop, Mr Botticelli started in on us.

'You kids eat those things outside! I don't want you dripping that stuff all over my floor!' he said as we got the Sunnyboys out of the freezer. So we all went and waited in the doorway while Tony paid for them and waited for his change. Only Mr Botticelli didn't give him any!

He reckoned it was owed to him for the sherbet dips he says we stole from him last week. There's no point trying to argue with Mr Botticelli and I was pretty sure that Tony had nicked those sherbet dips the last time we came in, so it was all fair.

When we got outside, I saw that Darren had wandered off. He does that sometimes, often chasing a pigeon or talking to some person and just walking off with them. It drives me nuts and I am always telling him he will get us all into terrible trouble if he keeps doing it, but it's like he can't help himself sometimes.

This time we found him up on Darlinghurst Road, his face pressed against the window of one of the souvenir shops that line the more touristy parts of the Cross. He was staring in, looking at all the kangaroo skin purses and cheap plywood boomerangs that the shop keeper has on display.

The American tourists and sailors love to buy that rubbish to take back to their families across the seas. I don't know why they want toy koalas and snow globes with the Harbour Bridge in them. It never snows in Sydney and you are more likely to see a rat or a cockroach than a koala around here. If they had to have a souvenir of real King's Cross wildlife, they should get a toy black-and-white ibis. At least you occasionally spotted one of them, or a grey brushtail possum scavenging through the garbage bins in the Domain.

Darren really wanted one of those snow globes. He was obsessed, even though we didn't have any money to buy one. He always stared at the one that had the city skyline painted on the back and the words *I wish I lived in Darlinghurst, Sydney* written in silvery glittery writing.

I pulled him away and took him home. I tried telling him that he could see the exact same thing in real life just by looking down the end of our street, but he still went on and on about that stupid snow globe and how pretty it was when the shop assistant shook it so all the snow fell.

20 JUNE 1973

School holidays have finally started and I am free of school for a whole week!

Mrs Frater gave us loads of homework, though. Fifth grade is way harder than fourth grade. The maths is the hardest and I can't seem to understand long division at all. But I am not going to spend my entire holidays trying to solve awful maths problems. This is our first really sunny day all winter, so I am not going to waste it being cooped up inside or writing much more in this journal.

27 JUNE 1973

I'm so bored. There's nothing to do and no money to do it with. No one wants to play on the street either because the thugs keep driving their Monaros up and down, yelling at us kids to get out of their way. We know they are friends of Pickaxe man because they all dress almost exactly like him, in fluorescent shirts and orange or red flared trousers. They all have mullets and moustaches, like it's some kind of mean thug uniform. Ma told us to ignore them, but if they ever tried to approach us to run to one of the neighbours quickly. Not as easy as it sounds now that there are so many empty houses on our side of the street and the people on the other side are mad at us and blame us for all the problems that are happening. I think they wish we would just all give up and move out so the thugs will go away and everything will be back to normal.

Only it won't be normal because there will be a great big ugly carpark right where our houses used to be. And what will stop anyone from doing the same to their houses and businesses? That's what I don't understand. This doesn't just affect us, it affects everyone in the whole street, the whole suburb, the whole country!

I found out Pickaxe man's name today. It's Mr Mangle and he definitely works for our landlord Mr Carson because I heard him talking to the Gattos this morning. He sounded real mean and told Mrs Gatto that they had to move out because if they didn't the house was going to be bulldozed right over them.

Mr Gatto got really mad and told Mangle to get out of his house and never come back.

Mangle just shrugged and said they would be moving out, one way or another.

7 JULY 1973

I saw Lucy yesterday. She was pushing down one of the fences which had been put up around number 91 and taking some groceries and furniture into the house. I thought this was a bit odd because I had seen all the tenants move out of there during the holidays after a whole lot of graffiti was scrawled across the doors and windows. The graffiti said nasty things like *Get Out Bludgers* and *You can't win.* After the tenants moved out, someone else added different graffiti which read, *Better to Squat than to let homes rot.*

Lucy saw me and waved and I asked her what she was doing. She explained she was setting up the house for a new group of squatters who were going to move in and stop the landlord from knocking it down.

I wondered why they would bother, now that all the people had left. It was just an empty house now.

Lucy didn't think it was, though. She said it was someone's home and a place that stored memories. This sounded like what Donnie's dad had said about the land, way back on Australia Day.

She said there is this thing called squatters rights which means that if someone is living in a building, even if they aren't the legal tenant, they can't be made to leave without going to court.

'That's how we are going to save all these houses,' Lucy said. 'We are going to stay in them until we get the heritage order. And the Builders' Labourers' are helping too. They have refused to do any demolition work anywhere on Victoria Street. We are going to save Victoria Street, Billie,' she said proudly. 'It worked in Woolloomooloo so it will work here."

I hope she is right, but more people seem to be leaving every week.

12 JULY 1973

Susie told me there were more bricks thrown through their windows last night and someone came over and stuffed their dunny full of newspaper that took ages to clear out. Susie has to use our toilet because theirs still isn't working properly.

Susie and her family are the last tenants in that whole house now. They had a few people move in a few weeks ago, but they moved out again really quickly.

I wish that mean Mangle man would leave my friend alone. If I see him, I'm going to tell him right to his ugly, stupid face!

18 JULY 1973

Me and the gang went up to Fitzroy Gardens after school today and hung around the fountain in the park. Not that it's really a park, like the Domain or Botanic Gardens.

It doesn't even have any grass or that many trees and it's right in the middle of Darlinghurst Road, with shops and clubs on either side of it, so it always smells like petrol fumes. It used to be a better park before someone decided to concrete and brick the whole thing and get rid of all the grass. I liked the grass even though there wasn't much of it because so many people walked through here to get to Bayswater Road. It was always muddy and slippery in winter and a total dustbowl in summer. But at least it was a bit of greenery, which is hard to find around here aside from the trees on our street. The rest of the Vic Street kids like it better now, though, because it's easier to ride roller skates and skateboards on it.

The Dandelion Fountain is right in the middle of the park and has been here for as long as I can remember. It's really named the El Alamein Fountain after a place in Egypt where Australian soldiers fought during World War Two, but all the locals just call it the Dandelion Fountain because that's exactly what it looks like—a huge steel dandelion shooting water out in all directions across a hexagon-shaped pool that is shallow enough to wade across on a hot day. I don't like the fountain much because it's always full of filthy water, cigarette butts and floating rubbish. Today it was too cold to go wading even if we wanted to, which me and Susie definitely didn't. Tony and Jacko decided they were going to be real drongos and jumped right in, shoes and all, and began splashing us with the filthy grey water. The coldness of it soaking through my green cardigan made me shiver.

Pretty soon we were all in a huge water fight, drenching each other and anyone else unfortunate enough to be anywhere near us. It was kind of fun until Darren fell in and got totally wet through.

I took him home to dry off, but Ma saw him all soaking wet and she was not at all happy. I know I am in for it as soon as she gets Darren out of the bath.

19 JULY 1973

Ma was convinced we were going to die from the water in the Dandelion Fountain, even though everyone knows anyone stupid enough to swallow that water would have to move into the outside dunny because they would be sick for weeks afterwards. There was no way I would have swallowed any.

But Ma wasn't going to take any chances and she dragged us down to St Vincent's hospital in our pyjamas and we spent almost the whole night waiting to see someone to tell us we weren't going to die.

I hate the hospital; it always smells like disinfectant and boiled cabbage. And there is nothing to do but sit on the uncomfortable plastic chairs and wait and wait and wait. Finally, a cross-looking nurse let us into the little curtained cubicle and asked why we were there. I tried to tell her that we didn't swallow any of the water, but she wasn't interested in listening any more than Ma was.

Ma also told her how I often run around the streets barefoot even though she has told me a million times I have to wear my shoes. And then Darren told her about how he had found a dead rat in one of the alleyways a few days ago and had believed it was a kitten until I had managed to get it away from him and thrown it into the bin. I really wish Darren had kept his mouth shut about that because I hadn't told anyone, and now Ma looked really cross. The nurse looked super worried and went and got a doctor, who decided both me and Darren needed to have a really painful tetanus injection—right in the tush!

It still hurts so bad that I couldn't even sit down at my desk at school and I have to lie on my stomach to write in this journal.

22 JULY 1973

My bottom still hurts a little bit, and it has been a raining constantly, so I have been stuck inside doing homework and feeling sorry for myself all weekend, Finally, around lunchtime, I took Darren over to Susie's to see if we could watch some TV. But the television wasn't getting any reception because of the weather, so we had to settle for playing some of Sherry's records instead.

I like 'Can the Can' by Susie Quatro and we played that until Sherry came in and roused on us and told us to stop. So I'm just going to fill in some of this journal because I haven't written anything in here for a while.

There are fleas jumping all over the place here at Susie's. It's not her fault—there are fleas almost everywhere on Victoria Street this year. They were much worse in summer and even our house had them, but luckily only on the lower floor and not up in our room. Mrs Gatto made a spray out of garlic, vinegar and water and sprayed it everywhere. The fleas do seem to have gone, but the whole downstairs smells of garlic all the time now and I'm not sure what's worse.

Susie's mum hasn't used any garlic spray, instead she has put out buckets of water for us to drop the little dead bodies in after we have caught and decapitated them. I am pretty good at catching them, but I'm still getting bitten a lot. As soon as the rain stops, we are going to go outside and look for some of the collectable bottle tops Darren is obsessed with. He has almost all the Peanuts characters now and we just need to find a Lucy Van Pelt one to complete his collection. She's meant to be the hardest one to find, and we have been looking for ages, but Darren really wants to have them all and it gives us something to do.

Oh, the rain has stopped. I am out of here!

LATER

We didn't find any bottle tops, but we did run into Miss Jane which was even better.

Miss Jane lives down at the Darlinghurst Road end of Vic Street. Everyone knows that she is some kind of royalty or heiress or something. Even though she has a lot of money, she isn't stuck up or mean. She's always nice to us kids, giving us lollies or, more often, pens and books for school. I've also seen her give Ma cash sometimes, when we can't make our rent or need groceries, although Ma always insists on trying to pay her back.

Even in the dirty laneway, Miss Jane looks glamorous, like one of those models in a fashion magazine that they sell on the main street. Today her black hair was piled up like a fancy cupcake on top of her head and she was wearing a blouse that looked like it was silk or something else expensive. I wish I could look like she does, but my hair is always tangled and I don't have any clothes that are as nice as hers.

Miss Jane didn't see us at first because she was staring at a poster that had been plastered up on one of the buildings. From where I stood, I could see it said ***Stop the Commos*** in heavy black type and under that there were some other words too small for me to read. There were lots of posters like that plastered up all over Challis Avenue, Victoria Street and in all the laneways and, to be honest, I never really thought about them. But they sure had upset Miss Jane because she ripped the poster down, scrunching it up and throwing it into a nearby skip bin. Then she saw us and she didn't look cross anymore. She smiled and asked us how we were. I told her we were looking for bottle tops with Lucy from Peanuts on them and she said she would help us look if we liked. It was nice of her, but I can't imagine someone like Miss Jane being any good at rummaging through gutters and garbage cans, pulling the linings out of bottle tops!

Darren loves Miss Jane and he's always smiling and taking her hand whenever he sees her. She seems to really like him, too, so I think she might have helped us if we had asked her to, but it was getting late and I didn't think there were many more bins we hadn't already searched.

Miss Jane said that she would keep an eye out and if she saw any bottle tops she would make sure to check for a Lucy under the lid. Darren then picked up the poster Miss Jane had thrown away and looked at it curiously.

'What's a Commo?' he asked.

At first Miss Jane hesitated, but then she said that commo was a slang term for a communist and that a communist is someone who thinks that the wealth of the people should be owned and shared out by the government.

I knew what a communist was. The Russians who had invaded Ma's country were communists and we were in something called a 'cold war' with them. I was suddenly a bit frightened because the posters made it seem like there were some right here, living on our street.

But Miss Jane said that communists weren't all bad people and some of the things they believed in were good, like fairness for all and the rich not being able to take everything from the poor.

It sounded to me like maybe Miss Jane was a communist, although that didn't make any sense because Miss Jane was one of the rich people, so I was a bit confused.

Miss Jane told us she wasn't a communist, she was a socialist, which she said was a different thing.

The way she explained it is that communists believe that everyone should be exactly equal and that the government should have absolute power over everything. But socialists believe that people should be treated fairly and look after each other and the environment we all live in but should also be able to live their lives as they wish. They should be able to have businesses and nice things, as long as they weren't getting those things by making the poor people suffer. She reckons our Prime Minister Gough Whitlam is a socialist. He is making sure we all get free healthcare and welfare for people who are not able to work, but he doesn't stop anyone from being whatever they want to be. I know my ma likes the Prime Minister a lot because on election day she took us down to the Domain and we handed out how-to-vote cards for him and she cried and cheered when he got voted in. I suppose if he is a socialist, she won't mind that Miss Jane is a socialist, too.

Miss Jane said Gough Whitlam is a good guy, but you can't totally rely on the government to look out for people all the time. Sometimes the government forgets about the poor people and women and migrants and Aboriginal people. Or they get greedy and help the rich people get richer, even if it makes everything worse for everyone in the end. She also said that a lot of people in Australia look down on working people and poor people, which I know is true because they are always calling us ratbags or dole bludgers in the papers, even though we never do anything except try to live the best way we can. Miss Jane says that the system is stacked in favour of the rich people and it's important that other people work to bring more balance because working people like my ma and the Gattos and Susie's dad don't have very much, even though they work really hard. Which isn't very fair.

I think that's true. My ma does work very hard every day, but we hardly have any money. But Tommo Jenkins's dad, who just sits around doing nothing much, has a big house and a new Ford Torino that he roars up and down the Cross, keeping all of the Eastern Suburbs up half the night.

That definitely wasn't fair or looking out for everyone, particularly those of us who needed to get some sleep.

I like talking to Miss Jane because she always listens to us kids and makes us feel like what we are saying is important. I asked her what I had to do to be a socialist and she said all it takes is believing that all people deserve equal rights and opportunities. I think I have always believed that, so I have been a socialist all along and didn't even know it!

I told Miss Jane about the thugs picking on Susie and her family and how that wasn't fair either because Susie hadn't done anything bad to them. Miss Jane said that Susie's parents should join the Victoria Street Action Group or at least come along to the meeting they were having to find out what could be done. She gave us some flyers she had in her purse to give to our parents.

Then she asked if we had the time to drop off more flyers around the neighbourhood for her. She would pay us twenty cents each.

Twenty cents! Of course we had the time!

So next week the three of us are going to Miss Jane's to pick up the flyers.

I'm already thinking about what I might spend my twenty cents on!

3 AUGUST 1973

This morning I saw inside Miss Jane's house. I expected it to be like a palace or a mansion or something, but it was pretty much exactly the same as all the other houses on Victoria Street—big and old and packed with people, mostly musicians, artists and students. All of them were busy running around or painting big banners or answering the cream-coloured phone that rang constantly in the hallway.

Miss Jane introduced us to a woman with a pretty, round face and dark hair whose name was Wanda, and a man called Johnny who brought us into a room piled high with stacks of flyers, all bundled into what looked like skyscrapers of paper.

I was worried we were expected to deliver all of the piles and piles of papers, but Johnny said that most of them were for a protest they were doing up in The Rocks the following weekend.

The Rocks is a place on the other side of the harbour and they are having the same problems with landlords trying to throw them out and bulldoze their houses, just like here. Only their landlords are the government, not Mr Carson.

I wasn't sure why people from the Victoria Street Action Group were going all the way over to the other side of the city when they should be focusing on the problems here.

When I asked Miss Jane, she asked me why Mick's friends from down at the docks came up to help Mick get his flat back from the thugs.

I wasn't quite so sure about that answer, but I reckoned it was because Mick and Mrs Fowler needed help and there was no-one else to help them.

'That's right, Billie. Just like when you saw Mrs Fowler on the street all alone and you helped her. Because you knew she needed it and you didn't know if anyone else was coming to help.'

I nodded. None of the other neighbours helped Mrs Fowler at all, except for Lucy who wasn't even a real resident, just a squatter, so I can kind of see what Miss Jane means. The people in The Rocks are like Mrs Fowler—they need help and so it's the right thing to do to help them.

That made me feel a bit bad about taking money for helping Miss Jane, but she just laughed and said that was okay because we were helping each other.

Then she gave us all our twenty cents, even though we hadn't delivered the flyers yet. It felt good to be trusted like that and we are not going to let Miss Jane down—we are going to spend all day tomorrow delivering the flyers to every letterbox in Darlinghurst!

7 AUGUST 1973

We still have heaps of flyers left over, even though Susie and Darren and I have spent the last three days trying to deliver them. It's not as easy as I thought it would be.

In fact, it was kind of depressing. We could see how many of the houses on our side of the street were empty, boarded off with big **NO TRESPASSING** signs in red and yellow stuck to the chain-link fencing or spray painted on the outside walls.

All the big men with their bigger moustaches were standing around watching us as we pushed flyers through letterboxes or left them on front steps or slipped them under doorways. Sometimes they took the flyers we had left behind and ripped them up right in front of us.

We kept on, though, sometimes handing the papers directly to the people who were sitting on their front steps or chatting on the sidewalks. Mostly those people just dropped them on the ground with barely a glance or threw them in the bin without reading them. Sometimes, when they did read them, they called us filthy commos.

I tried to tell them we weren't commos, we were socialists, but they just laughed at us or moved away with disgusted looks on their faces.

I don't know why so many people were annoyed about a few flyers. They didn't say anything much on them anyway, just the words '**Victoria Street Action Group Public Meeting, SAVE OUR STREET**' and the date of the meeting which was happening in a few days at Wayside Chapel.

Honestly, if it had been for anyone else, I would have given up and tipped all the flyers into one of the skips behind the pub. But Miss Jane had trusted us to deliver every one of the flyers and paid us a lot of money to do it, so I can't let her down.

We'll do the rest of them tomorrow.

8 AUGUST 1973

I saw Pickaxe again today!

Darren had wanted a chocolate Billabong, so me, Susie and Darren walked up to Mr Botticelli's shop, thinking we could drop some more of Miss Jane's flyers in the houses and flats on Challis Street on the way.

But as we were walking, Pickaxe came and tried to grab the flyers off us.

He was really scary with his big wooden stick and wolfish face. And when he grinned at me, I saw he had no front teeth, just a big black gap where his front teeth should have been. It was the scariest face I had ever seen—but we didn't give into him.

He told me that it was no use and that we weren't going to change anything with a few flyers and a stupid meeting. But if that was true, why was he so worried about us handing them out? He even offered me twenty cents to throw all the flyers in the bin. But I told him to rack off and then Susie, Darren and I ran into Mr Botticelli's shop to try to get away from him.

Usually, Mr Botticelli wouldn't let us hang around in there, but he saw Pickaxe through the glass front door, tearing up the flyers he had snatched from us, and Mr Botticelli said we could eat our Billabongs right there by the counter.

Darren even dripped chocolate ice cream on the floor and Mr Botticelli didn't get mad or anything.

Then Pickaxe tried to come into the store and Mr Botticelli told him get out! Told him if he kept hanging around scaring kids, he would call the coppers.

I knew that wouldn't do any good cause the coppers don't seem to care what Pickaxe and his thugs do. But Pickaxe might not have known that because he walked away without saying anything.

I always thought Mr Botticelli hated us Vic Street kids—we did call him Mr Bottom-Celli behind his back and sometimes even to his face. But today Mr Botticelli showed himself to be a real cool cat.

He even took a couple of our flyers and stuck them up in his window for everyone to see.

I think this is even better than putting them in letterboxes.

10 AUGUST 1973

Good news! Miss Jane spoke to Mick about what was

happening at Susie's house and he organised a whole load of people to go in and squat in the other flats in Susie's building.

No-one will be game to attack Susie's house now that there are ten or so young blokes and sheilas ready to fight back.

Susie told me that when the thugs did turn up to harass them last night, all the squatters scared them off with a whole lot of old firecrackers Sherry had saved from the Queen's birthday weekend. Susie and Sherry even joined in, tipping a bucket of water and flour over two thugs who were banging on their door at three in the morning!

I wish I had been there!

Anyway, the good news is that Susie's mum and dad are happy to stay there now, at least while the squatters are there, so Susie and her TV are here to stay, I reckon!

14 AUGUST 1973

Today when we got home from school, Ma was standing out the front of our house in her work uniform talking with Pickaxe man! Ma was frowning and her arms were crossed tightly across her chest while that mean old Mangle was leaning right over our low front fence saying something to her that I couldn't hear, the wooden handle dangling from his right hand, clinking against the wrought iron.

I could see that Pickaxe was doing his best to intimidate her, but all he was really doing was making her mad. And you don't want to see my ma when she gets mad. That I know from experience.

Pickaxe didn't seem to realise he was playing with fire, though, and kept trying to grab my mum's arm. She pulled away from him and hit him hard with her bag, right across his chin.

That's when she saw Darren and me walking towards her. She tried to smile and told us just to stay where we were. I grabbed hold of Darren and held him still as my ma turned back to Pickaxe and put her face right up against his so they were almost nose to nose with only the fence between them.

I heard Ma say to Pickaxe, 'Get out of here now. I have paid my rent; I have a lease. We both know you can't legally make us leave and you are not going to bully us out. I have stood up to worse bullies than you, so get out of my face!'

Mangle must have seen something in Ma's eyes because he stepped back really quickly, although he pretended he wasn't bothered.

'Just being friendly,' he said in a deep rumbling voice. 'Just letting you know what's what.'

He then turned to Darren and me and gives us the creepiest smile I ever did see.

I took a step back, putting my hands defensively around Darren's shoulders.

'This is no place to raise kids, ma'am,' Pickaxe said, still looking directly at me and Darren. 'You'd do well to take the offer I am making you seriously.'

Then with one last look at all of us, he ambled away.

He didn't go far, though, just across the street where he stopped in the shade of a tree, watching as Darren ran into Mum's arms.

Mum hugged Darren and me and took us inside, but I noticed she never took her eyes off the man across the road. She didn't go to work that night either.

18 AUGUST 1973

Today Miss Jane gave us some more flyers and another twenty cents each!

This time she wanted us to take them down to the Wayside Chapel in Hughes Street and give them to Reverend Ted who would hand them out to anyone who visited the chapel, the soup kitchen or the op shop.

The Wayside Chapel has been part of the Cross for as long as I can remember and everyone on Victoria Street knows Rev Ted who runs the place.

I think everyone who was born in the street was christened at Wayside, even me and Darren and my ma isn't even religious. Darren and I get most of our clothes from the charity drives Wayside does every year; last year Rev Ted even gave Darren a proper recorder from the donations. Ma took it off him right smart because the sound of that awful whistling was enough to make you go barmy!

Of course, Rev Ted knew all about the Victoria Street Action Group meeting and said it was good that people were standing up to the bullies because what was happening in Vic Street just wasn't right. He said that the way they had treated poor old Arnold, grabbing him and taking him away like that was terrible. I didn't know who Arnold was, or what had happened to him, but Rev Ted seemed to realise he shouldn't have said anything, and refused to tell us anymore. He quickly changed the subject and said he was going to go and get a couple of dresses Susie and I might like from the donation bin.

While we were waiting, Susie poured us some green lime cordial and we slurped it down. Handing out flyers is thirsty work!

That's when I saw Pa, sitting out in the chapel's garden. He was cleaned up a bit now, his beard washed and brushed through. He was still wearing that filthy green coat, though.

I figured he was just there for a wash and a hot meal until I saw who he was sitting next to. Our archenemy—Pickaxe! Both of them were sitting there chatting away like mates.

Of course, my pa will talk to anyone who gives him a drink and I don't care who he hangs about with usually. But it was weird. Why would a thug like Pickaxe waste his time sitting around Wayside Chapel talking to a loser like my pa?

The whole thing seemed wrong and slightly dangerous somehow.

They were both gone by the time Rev Ted came back with the clothes and I was so excited by the pink floral dress—only a bit too big for me—I forgot to ask Rev Ted if he often saw Pickaxe hanging around.

21 AUGUST 1973

Susie and I have been hanging out with Lucy and some of the women who are squatting in the abandoned house in our street. They are really cool. We were playing jump rope in the street when they invited us to join them for a picnic on the lawn of number 115. They always seemed to be together in groups, sitting on balconies or front steps or even on the street curbs of the squats; having picnics and singing songs. I felt really grown up and important joining them.

They even shared their food with us—proper sandwiches with roast beef and chutney on them—not the tomato sauce sandwiches we usually eat.

Lucy seems to have moved into one of the other flats in 115 permanently now. She took us inside and we saw that they have turned Mick and Mrs Fowler's flat into a bit of an activity centre, full of people making banners and playing music. Outside, there is even a place where us kids can hang out and play. It has a set of swings and heaps of toys and activity books. The whole place seems full of kids now, though most of them are a bit younger than me. Lucy says the kids belong to a lot of the people who are moving in to help save the street, as well as kids from all over Darlo who just like hanging out here.

I can't wait to tell Ma all about it because it would be a great place for Darren and me to hang out when she is at work.

I really like Lucy and the others. Most of them are students from Sydney University, which means they are all really smart. She reckons I could go to university one day if I want to, now that our Prime Minister has got rid of university fees. I never thought about that before, but I am good at school and have got good marks for everything I have done.

Lucy's friends are in a gang just like us. They call themselves the Sydney Push. I asked Lucy if they had named themselves after the Darlinghurst Push that Tilly Devine had run in the 1930s. Lucy was really impressed that I knew about that and so I told her all about the heritage project I did for school and how I had learned all about the history of the street. Lucy said Susie and I were definitely smart enough to study at university, just like she did, and maybe become historians or something. I'm not sure about that because I still like the idea of being a builders' labourer. Maybe I could do both?

Lucy also said we could become honorary members of the Push, even though we weren't at university or anything. So now I am part of two great gangs: the Vic Street gang and the Sydney Push! And together we are going to stop Pickaxe man and his thugs and the mean landlord who pays them to scare us and steal our houses from under us.

~

23 AUGUST 1973

I knew Pa was up to no good with that Pickaxe man. Today he turned up suddenly on our landing and I know Pickaxe is behind it somehow.

I had been playing at Susie's most of the afternoon and when I came back home, I saw Ma and Pa yelling at each other on the stairs.

Mrs Finnegan was watching the whole thing through her door, but I could see by her expression she had been too scared to come out and do anything about it.

Mrs Finnegan is a mousy, shy woman. She is also tiny, as small as her eldest child and he's only nine. Mrs Finnegan has lived here for three years and I like her well enough. We hardly ever saw Mr Finnegan because he goes up north to find work a lot of the time, leaving Mrs Finnegan and the kids to pretty much fend for themselves.

When she saw me looking at her, she closed the door

quickly but then opened it again a moment later, her brown eye peering out. She probably thought I hadn't noticed.

Pa was yelling at my ma in a mixture of English and German, his face so red and flushed I thought he looked like a tomato. I remembered how he always used to do that, his German accent making him sound even more threatening.

My ma never backed down, though.

'You aren't coming in here, Wilhelm!' she yelled back.

Ma and Pa didn't notice me standing on the stairs as they fought because Pa was trying really hard to get into our room and Ma was trying just as hard to stop him. It didn't matter how many times Ma stepped up to bar the way, though, or told him to get lost. My pa was not giving up.

After his third attempt to get past my ma, Pa's face changed expression and he became all childlike and whiny. 'Please let me in and we talk about it, ja?' Pa pleaded. 'You know how much I miss you.'

I couldn't figure out why my pa was back.

Then, as if to answer that very question, my pa said, 'And I need that money, Elena, we both do.'

Of course, that was why he was here. But he was barking up the wrong tree because my ma sure didn't have any money to spare, especially now she wasn't working as many shifts at

Harry's so she could be home at nights with us in case the thugs came around.

Then I remembered that I still had my savings hidden in a jar under our bed. I was saving up to buy some second-hand roller skates I had seen at the pawn brokers up on Macleay Street. They were five dollars and it would take me ages to save up, but with the money Miss Jane had given me and the coins I had made collecting aluminium cans, I was closer to buying them than I had ever been.

I couldn't let Pa just go in and take my life savings!

I wanted to go up and help Ma keep him out, but I didn't want to leave Darren on the stairs by himself and Ma seemed to be doing a good job stopping Pa all by herself, so I watched and waited, ready to jump in if Ma looked like she needed me.

'You have no right to it even if I do take it!' Ma said, pushing him away from the doorway.

'We could go away together. Just you and me, like old times. It's a fresh start!' Pa said, which seemed really odd. Why would my ma want to go anywhere with him? And where would me and Darren be if they did?

Of course, Ma wasn't going to leave us and certainly not for him. My pa is mad, he really is, and she told him so.

'If you don't do what I say, I'm not responsible for what

I do,' Pa said then, his fists clenching by his sides.

'Don't you threaten me, Wilhelm!' Ma yelled back, looking him square in the eye. They were almost the same height, though my ma has more than a few pounds on him.

Just then the downstairs apartment door creaked open and I looked down to see Mr Gatto come out and stand at the foot of the stairwell, looking up at me and Darren with a question in his eyes. He was wrapped up in his old dressing-gown and it was clear he had been disturbed from his usual evening paper, which he still held in his hand.

He called up and asked if Ma was all right.

My pa came over and looked down at Mr Gatto and his red face paled. I knew Mr Gatto wouldn't hurt a fly, but all my pa saw was a big, hulking Italian man with hands the size of frying pans and an irritated expression on his face. Pa dropped his fists and gave Ma a hard look.

'You got no right, Elena. Keeping a man from his fortune.'

He turned and staggered drunkenly towards where we were standing. I didn't think he even saw us as he pushed past, but then suddenly he grabbed my wrist and pulled me towards him.

'You need your papa, don't ya, fräulein?' he slurred, hugging me so close I was enveloped in the stink of his sweat.

I pulled away, disgusted, as Darren stood ignored beside me.

But then Mr Gatto was on the stairs and he said in his deep, baritone voice, 'You go now, mister, before there is trouble.'

Pa glared at Mr Gatto, but he released me, turned on his heel and stumbled down the stairs, snorting at Darren who was standing still and frightened on the landing.

I thought about pushing him down the stairs at that moment, a terrible thought, I know. And I would never have really done it. But I can't lie and say I wasn't tempted. As if reading my thoughts, Pa tripped slightly on the middle step but righted himself at the last moment, defying gravity the way drunks always seemed able to do.

He gave us all one last sneer before Mr Gatto led him out, an expression on our neighbour's face that even a mean drunk like my pa wasn't going to mess with.

I never will understand why my ma married my pa in the first place. But Ma said that my pa wasn't always a bad man. That when they first met, he had been funny and handsome and had promised her the world. It was only later when the drink and bookies got to him that he became the father I knew.

I wish I knew the man he was before; I don't have any memories of that. Just memories of him yelling or falling asleep drunk. Or leaving.

1 SEPTEMBER 1973

Oh, how I hate to write this. The Gattos are leaving!

Mr Gatto told Ma today, during dinner.

All of them are going, even Tony the Cat!

Mr Gatto said they are going to move to a flat above the shop where he works.

Tony doesn't want to go because he says it stinks of fish and old cooking oil. But Mr Gatto is determined to take them all.

I can't believe it. I really can't. The Gattos have lived in this house as long as us. Longer probably. Ever since Mr and Mrs Gatto came over from Italy after the Second World War.

I can't imagine the house without them in it.

Mr Gatto kept saying that it was because he would be closer to work. But Mrs Gatto looked really sad and I knew why they were really leaving. They're scared.

Things have gotten bad here.

A lot of the other residents have been scared away and there aren't enough people to squat in the houses that have already been abandoned. Houses have been vandalised. People have been hurt in the street. Everyone knows about it.

Mr Gatto said the money the developer was offering was a good deal and it was silly to keep holding out.

'We think maybe you should go, too,' he told my ma. 'They are going to move everyone out anyway.'

But Ma wasn't having any of it. She said she was sorry that the Gattos were going and she would miss them. But we were staying right where we were.

'I don't give into bullies, Alberto, even ones with big wads of cash.'

Mr Gatto was going to say something to Ma when she said that, but Ma didn't give him a chance. She just hustled us up from the dining table and made us go to our room.

It's not fair!

I just find out Susie is staying, but now I am losing Tony the Cat.

The world can play cruel jokes, don't you think?

7 SEPTEMBER 1973

Another terrible thing has happened!

Yesterday a house in Victoria Street burned to the ground.

It was only a few doors away from us. The police told the papers that it was empty, but everyone knows there were people squatting in there. A man and a woman from out bush.

Ma said the woman didn't get out and died in the fire. No-one here seems to know her name.

I had seen her go into the house. She was only young, younger than Miss Jane. Hardly anyone in the street knew her. Her brother jumped out the window to escape the fire, that's what I heard, and he's been taken to the hospital. Ma said the police are blaming him for the fire because he's an Aborigine. I don't think he did it. I think it was the thugs. I reckon that's what everyone on the street thinks, too. But the police aren't listening to any of us and continue to do nothing about the goons who are still walking around threatening us.

Everyone here is really scared now. Miss Maude and Miss Millie have left and Mr Ted moved his things across the street to the boarding house. I don't really miss any of them, but when the Gattos leave the place will really feel empty.

10 SEPTEMBER 1973

The Gattos moved out yesterday.

Any doubts they would leave were gone after that fire happened.

Ma decided to forgive them, though, and she threw them a big going-away party with us and the Finnegans and Susie and her family.

The whole house was filled with tearful goodbyes and lots of promises to write and keep in touch.

Susie even gave Tony the Cat a kiss, right on the mouth. I bet he's sorry he's leaving now!

Then they were gone. Their apartment is empty now except for the cheap sticks of furniture and worn rugs that were there before they moved in.

It was weird going into their old flat and not seeing Mrs Gatto's big crucifixes or the framed photo of Ernesto looking down from above them.

I borrowed one of Susie's permanent markers and we drew a replacement of Ernesto in the spot where his photo had always been. It didn't really look like him, though. His nose was too big and I think I made him a bit cross eyed by accident.

Ma saw it and yelled at me, saying I shouldn't be

vandalising property. She doesn't understand. It's not vandalising, it's a memorial.

15 SEPTEMBER 1973

Today there was no sign of the Finnegans. They just up and disappeared. We didn't even see them go.

Now all the rooms in the house are empty except for ours.

I never thought I would miss all the noise of those Finnegan kids, or the wet bathroom and their dirty dishes in the downstairs sink.

But I do.

20 SEPTEMBER 1973

Pickaxe has turned up at our house three times since all our neighbours left.

It's not enough he scared the Gattos and the Finnegans away. Now he is determined to get us out, too.

Ma never opens the door when he comes around, but I don't think he's giving up.

22 SEPTEMBER 1973

Today we woke up to find curse words scrawled on our front door in red spray paint.

The three of us scrubbed away at them for hours. But no matter how hard we scrubbed, we couldn't get them off. Finally, Ma sent me and Darren down to the store to buy a tin of white paint.

Ma painted over the dull pink words because she said even if the paint didn't match, it was better than coming home every day to see those words written about us. That new patch of white does look odd, though—almost illuminated next to the dull, grey, peeling paint of the rest of the doorway.

10 OCTOBER 1973

Ma took us to the residents' Action meeting today. There have been meetings every week since January, at Wayside Chapel or in one of the houses and sometimes right on the street, but this was the first time Ma had agreed to go to one.

Ma has started to be more friendly to the squatters and the Action Group since the Gattos moved out. People from the Sydney Push have been coming around to check on us quite often and give us food and money. Ma got fired from Harry's because she couldn't do night shifts anymore, so we don't have much money for food and stuff. She did get a job at the restaurant up on Darlinghurst Road, but she only gets a few day shifts a week now. She still makes sure she pays our rent, though, every single week. She says as long as she does that, we are still legal tenants.

Ma really likes Miss Jane and she lets us hand out her flyers and even take part in some of the protests that are held on the street every couple of days. But only the ones on a weekend because we aren't allowed to miss school.

I was really excited to go to the meeting. I thought it would be a big hub of activity like it is at Jane or Mick's house. But it was just a load of people sitting in chairs and listening as other people talked about what was happening in the street. No-one seemed happy and there was a lot of arguing and muttering going on.

The speakers mainly talked about boring things like court cases and legal action. But when they asked for volunteers to help patrol the empty houses and stop the thugs from breaking in and stealing things or wrecking the places, Susie, Jacko and I were the first to volunteer.

They said we were a bit too young, but we could keep an eye out on our way to school and when we were playing and let the proper patrol members know if we saw anything. It wasn't quite as cool, but at least Ma agreed to that.

A lot of the thugs were at the meeting, too, which I don't think should have been allowed. They were mostly sitting in the back of the hall, jeering and yelling insults and generally trying to be scary whenever someone was trying to talk.

So, the meeting wasn't really as fun as I hoped it would be, though Darren, Susie, Jacko and I did get to eat as many Milk Arrowroots and drink as much lime cordial as we wanted while the grownups all talked and argued and passed resolutions.

I didn't recognise all the people there, except for some of the older neighbours who are still refusing to move out, like Mr Stanislav and of course Susie's mum and dad who were there with the baby. Sherry even turned up with her latest hippie boyfriend.

Most of the front row was taken up by people who I knew from the Sydney Push, all in their black or dark clothing, ignoring the thugs up the back. Lucy and Wanda were there, as well as Johnny and the three young students who had moved into rooms in Susie's house. They greeted us with a hug when we arrived and seemed very pleased that Ma had finally decided to attend. Ma sat with Susie's parents and I saw the three of them look a bit confused when suddenly everyone else stood up and started clapping as a short man with curly brown hair stepped out the front to talk to the crowd.

I had never seen him before, but everyone from the Push and the Action Group seemed to know who he was.

He introduced himself as Jack Mundey and said he was one of the leaders of the BLF. Everyone started clapping even louder when he said that, and I joined right in. The BLF was the main reason why the developers had lost in Woolloomooloo and were losing here in Victoria Street and in The Rocks, so we all wanted to give him a hero's welcome—except the thugs up the back, who started booing and cursing at him.

But they were drowned out by the BLF supporters. Eventually, everyone was quiet, and Jack Mundey spoke. He was a happy man with a wide smile and he didn't seem worried at all about the mean men at the back of the hall who were still hissing and booing him. In fact, he even addressed them, some by name, and said he was glad they were there giving their support to the BLF and the action group by attending the meeting, which made everyone laugh because we all knew that was not what these thugs were there for at all.

Jack then reminded everyone that when the residents had asked for a green ban on the houses of Victoria Street back in April, the BLF had agreed and that another green ban had led to work stopping down in Woolloomooloo and at The Rocks and in Centennial Park. Here in Vic Street, the green ban was giving residents time to get their own cases heard in court or have the houses heritage listed and stop the threat to our houses before it got as far as the bulldozers coming in. He said he had spoken to Mr Carson who had assured everyone that he would not evict any more residents until the court cases had been decided.

I saw a lot of the Sydney Push shake their heads and scoff at this because we all knew the thugs were still trying to get people out. But Jack Mundey urged everyone to be positive.

'We can win here!' he said loudly. 'Just as we won in Woolloomooloo, just as we are winning in The Rocks and just as we won in Kelly's Bush. We just have to stay strong. Mr Carson and our Premier, Mr Askin, may not realise it, but this city of Sydney is for everyone, not just the rich and powerful. And the BLF will make sure none of you have your homes torn down around you.'

The people from the Push clapped and whistled and called out in approval, but the thugs in the hall were angry and told Jack Mundey to get out of their street.

Their street! None of them even lived here!

The thugs got up and started throwing chairs around and even tipped over the table near us which had all the biscuits and lime cordial laid out, spilling everything all over the floor. People started to leave, fearing that things were soon going to turn nasty, and Ma came running up and hustled all us kids out of the hall into the Wayside garden.

Behind us I heard chairs crashing and people yelling and I knew enough to know that a fight was going to break out if they didn't all calm down. Which was why Ma led us out onto Hughes Street, where more thugs were standing around, watching the people leave. Ma pulled us past them as fast as she could, towards home, but as we rushed past, I saw someone I recognised. My pa, standing right next to Pickaxe man, grinning and laughing. His beard was shaved off and he looked a lot cleaner than when I saw him last, but I am sure it was him.

I've decided not to mention it to Ma, though, because she has enough to worry about.

20 OCTOBER 1973

Today the Sydney Opera House officially opened and Ma, Darren and I, as well as all the Angelovs, plus a few other people from the street, walked down to Bennelong Point to watch all the festivities.

The place was totally packed, with people sitting on the stairs, the pavement and the railings. Mr Angelov got us a good spot and we were able to see all the processions and the navy display. They even had a load of helicopters fly right over us. The noise was so loud I thought my ears would burst.

Everyone in Sydney seemed to have come out for it and the day started with parades of all kinds of people in colourful clothes, with drums and pipes and all sorts of instruments I hadn't seen before. Ma identified each group for Darren as they passed. There were people who had travelled here all the way from Papua New Guinea, New Zealand and the Cook Islands, as well as marching rows of Greek, Italian and Croatian people who lived right in this city.

I was delighted to see some of the kids from the high school marching in the parade and I waved to them excitedly, but they didn't wave back. I guess I was hard to see in the crowd. Everyone looked so happy and important in their uniforms or fancy clothes, but my favourite was the group of ladies with flowers in their long dark hair who marched in skirts made of grass.

Mrs Angelov said they are from Hawaii and Polynesia. Exotic lands I had never heard of until today! Someday I am going to travel to all these places and find those beautiful ladies who marched today and thank them for coming here and making the day so special for us boring old Sydneysiders.

It was a great day except that thunder clouds gathered above us and a mighty wind tore up through Bennelong Point, snatching away hats and scarves from anyone who wasn't quick enough to grab them. Darren and I made a game out of trying to catch them as they cartwheeled or floated past us.

Raindrops didn't fall, though. Maybe because even Mother Nature knew it would be downright un-Australian to rain today, not when we were expecting the Queen of England herself to arrive any minute.

That's right! The actual Queen of England, Elizabeth the Second! The one we sing 'God Save the Queen' to at school every day. That's just to her portrait, though. Today I saw her in real life. Moving and talking and waving and everything!

She turned up in this big, expensive black car with two Union Jack flags on the front that fluttered in the wind. Everyone around us was so quiet, frightened they might scare her off if they even breathed. Even the storm clouds that had been threatening all morning cleared away and the sun came out and streamed light around them as the Queen and Prince Philip stepped out of the car.

She looked so beautiful in her pale blue dress and matching hat, though I have to say not quite as beautiful as the Polynesian girls looked in their grass skirts. I didn't say that out loud though, because Ma loved the Queen almost more than anything and I didn't want her to think I was being disrespectful.

I wanted to shake the Queen's hand like I had seen other little girls do on the newsreels. I had been practising my curtsey and everything. But she was too far away so I had to make do with just waving at her from the steps.

It was probably for the best because up close she might have noticed that my floral dress had a tomato sauce stain on it and my sandals were scuffed and the buckle was held on with a rubber band—though I knew she would never be rude enough to mention it.

The Queen took her seat and some bloke stood up and said a few words I couldn't really hear that well. I didn't know who he was, but I could hear some of the members of the Push booing him as he spoke. I knew it was them even from a distance because they were dressed as they usually were, in their black jeans and turtleneck sweaters.

Ma told me the man was Mr Askin, the Premier of New South Wales. That meant he made all the decisions about what happened in Sydney. I guess that is why the Push didn't like him, because they didn't like the way things were here. I don't think Mr Askin heard them booing because he was a long way away and the wind snatched away the catcalls the same way it had snatched the hats and scarves, sending the protests out into the harbour.

The Queen stood up and said a few words and then it was all over. The Opera House was officially opened. People swarmed down the steps, taking photos of the Opera House and the harbour and trying to get a picture with the Queen.

She was gone, though, whisked away in the big black car.

We all sat there for a minute, waiting for the crowds to clear. Ma was so happy, grinning at everyone. She said she never thought she would ever get to see the Queen up close like that. She wasn't that close, really. Her Majesty was easier to see on the telly in Susie's flat than she was from where we were sitting. But I didn't want to spoil Ma's mood. She hasn't been smiling much lately, so it was nice to see her so happy.

Mrs Angelov didn't look happy, though. She just stared out at the harbour until Ma asked her what was wrong.

'This is the end of it for us,' Mrs Angelov said.

'What do you mean?' Ma asked.

'You think now that they have this Opera House here on the harbour that they are going to continue to let people like us live anywhere near it?'

I noticed the storm clouds above us were gathering once again and I didn't think they were going to hold off this time.

'You mark my words, Elena,' Susie's mum continued, 'that's really why they are moving us out. Because we have too much of this—' she gestured towards the blue glittering water and the flotilla of expensive boats bobbing out on the harbour '—and it is worth too much to people like them.'

'Don't be silly,' Ma said, brushing off Mrs Angelov's

words. 'It's just an opera house. Once the Queen has gone home, people will lose interest in it. It's very odd-looking and silly, really. The harbour is for everybody. Always has been. The Rocks were saved from developers, and Kelly's Bush on the other side of the harbour. And the BLF even stopped the Opera House itself, with its silly carpark, from destroying the Botanic Gardens. You don't have to worry; people won't support the crazy development and destruction of public land like the Premier thinks they will. And no right-minded person would support people's homes being destroyed and replaced by freeways and carparks.'

Mrs Angelov shook her head hotly and said no-one cared about people like us. She gestured to the crowds of brightly dressed men and women all laughing and taking photos. 'The papers are already blaming us Vic Street residents for slowing down progress. The daily newspapers are constantly calling us lazy criminals bludging off the country by staying in our own homes!'

She pulled a newspaper out of her bag and showed us the headline: **VICTORIA STREET SQUATTERS ILLEGAL ACTION.**

I didn't have a chance to read what it said, but Mrs Angelov told us the gist of it. She said that the squatters who had been trying to get the courts to allow them to stay had lost. The writer of the article didn't seem at all upset by this. But I was. And so, it seemed, was Susie's mum.

'You'll see,' she continued. 'Someone is going to get hurt. And for what? A road and a carpark and probably a bunch of offices looking out at an opera house in a city where most of us can't afford to even see the opera!'

'Are you giving up?' Ma asked suddenly, and even in all the noise and movement of the celebration, I felt the world go silent. I knew that whatever Mrs Angelov said next would affect me and Susie forever.

She looked sad. 'We've thought about it a lot. But we can't keep holding out. Carson turned off our power and our water; there's damage done to the house every night. They're threatening our daughters on the street. It just isn't a safe place for any of us anymore.'

'Come and move in with us,' Ma said. 'The room across the hall is empty now. Or you could take the Gatto's old flat. There's more than enough room for all of you there. We could hold out together.'

I reached for Susie and we hugged each other tightly, looking at Mrs Angelov with beseeching eyes.

She seemed to waver and I thought we had won.

Susie would be able to stay, all of us together at number 85!

But it was Mr Angelov who crushed our dreams.

'I'm sorry, Elena, Billie,' he said, pulling Susie away from my embrace. 'But you won't be able to hold out too much longer yourselves. There is violence waiting to happen on that street and I am not going to let my daughters be in the middle of it.'

Ma frowned, but Mrs Angelov nodded in agreement. 'You would do well to move you and your kids out as well, Elena. There's housing opening up on the outskirts of Sydney and on the Central Coast. Not as cheap as here, but some of it is by the sea and you can make a good life.'

Ma shook her head. 'You can't give in to bullies, Sophia,' she said coldly. 'Didn't we learn that in Europe? Once they see we are weak, they will never stop taking from us.'

Mrs Angelov looked a bit ashamed. But it passed in an instant and she picked up Angelica and turned away.

'This isn't Bulgaria or the Ukraine,' Mrs Angelov said. 'Here it is the capitalists who have all the power, and the outcome is the same. It doesn't matter how hard you fight, if they are powerful, you will lose. Sometimes the fight isn't worth it. We'll be moving out at the end of the week.' She turned her back on us as she grabbed a crying Susie with her free hand and dragged her away. Then they were engulfed in the sea of people and my best friend disappeared from view in the crush of the happy, singing crowd.

28 OCTOBER 1973

The day Susie and her family left was the saddest day in my whole life.

I cried and cried and hugged Susie so tightly I thought they would never be able to break us apart. I was losing my best friend because a load of yobbos was scaring her mum. And now she was going far away and I would most likely never see her again.

Susie promised to write and I know she will, and I will write, too. But it won't be the same. Not only am I losing my best friend ever, but they are taking the telly and everything.

No *Bewitched* on a rainy weekday afternoon, no *Skippy the Bush Kangaroo* and, worst of all, no dancing along to *Young Talent Time* on a Saturday night!

Those goons have taken everything from me now and I hate them more than I have ever hated anyone.

1 NOVEMBER 1973

Mrs Frater came up to our house today and Ma found out I had been skipping school. Mrs Frater said I had missed so much I was probably going to be held back in Grade Five if I didn't get myself sorted out. Ma was so mad and she yelled and yelled at me, right in front of my teacher.

But I don't care. Nothing matters anymore. It doesn't matter what you do or how hard you try, there are always people who will take everything away from you.

It wasn't even that much fun bunging off school. I still had to walk down to the infant school every day to drop off Darren. I couldn't go home because Ma might be there, so I wandered around, avoiding the main roads because Ma might also be out shopping or have picked up a shift in one of the restaurants she had applied to as a casual worker. Sometimes I hung out at Mick's house because there are loads of kids there now, coming in with the new squatters and activists who haven't given up, even though the court said they had to. But most of them are younger than me and aren't much fun to play with. I don't want to make any new friends anyway because they will all be forced to go away, too, or I will. And that will just make me sadder still.

On the weekends I just stay in our room, playing with Darren or reading my library books because I don't like leaving the house if I don't have to. I have nightmares all the time that I come home and our house is all boarded up and full of monsters in day-glo shirts leering at me through the windows.

When I told Ma and Mrs Frater all of that they were less mad at me for missing school, but Ma said I still had to go. Mrs Frater said that she would help me try to get my grades up and do everything she could to make sure I went on to Grade Six next year. But I really don't care.

I agreed to go back, though, because what else was there to do?

Before she left, Mrs Frater gave me a book, not a library one, but one I could keep. It's all about a bushranger called Ned Kelly. She said I might like to read it because reading about him might help me feel less alone.

She said Ned Kelly had a lot of worries, and I might find I had a bit in common with him. I don't know why she thought I had anything in common with a criminal! But I didn't have anything else left to read, so after she left, I read a bit of the Ned Kelly book and Mrs Frater was right. The book didn't really talk about bushranging at all. It talked about how hard life was for the poor people in Ned Kelly's time, like it is now.

Ned Kelly and his family were picked on by bullies, too—a bunch of coppers and rich people who took everything away from them and then punished them for stealing back what they could.

He lost everything, just like me, but he didn't give up, so maybe I shouldn't either.

I don't mean I am going to become a bushranger or anything. But I reckon if Ned Kelly was born in Victoria Street instead of Victoria and was living now instead of way back in the past, well, he would have been out there with Mick and Jane and the Sydney Push fighting to make sure those bullies didn't win.

And that's what I should be doing, too.

13 NOVEMBER 1973

Things in the street have settled down a bit.

I still miss Susie dreadfully, but maybe everything else is going to be okay. I went back to school and Mrs Frater has been true to her word and is helping me catch up on all the lessons I missed. I am still really bad at maths, but I am doing pretty well with all the other subjects and have done really well in history and English.

Ma, Darren and I are still holding on at number 85, but most of the neighbouring houses are empty now. None of the goons have been around bothering us for weeks, so maybe they have given up. Or maybe Mick and the others have finally won a court case.

I have even made a new friend. Her name is Jennie and she is one of the kids who moved in with some of the squatters. She and her mum are staying in one of the houses down the street. She isn't quite as cool as Susie and Tony, but she has a pair of rollerskates she lets me borrow sometimes. They are the same ones that I was going to buy, but I couldn't save up enough money in time and when I went to the shop last week, they were already sold.

I thought they were gone forever until I saw Jennie wearing them. I was really mad at first because those skates were supposed to be mine. I told her so, too, but instead of getting mad or being mean, Jennie just took off one of the skates and gave it to me and said we could both use them.

They are those open metal skates that tie around your shoes, so they fit anyone. But when we are only wearing one each we can't stay upright, even if we hold onto each other, and we just end up falling flat on our bums. So, we started taking turns with the skates and now we hang out together almost every day.

It's almost like having Susie back again. Except Jennie doesn't have a TV, but I suppose the rollerskates are almost as good.

15 NOVEMBER 1973

Our power went out last night.

Just suddenly, at about 10 pm, it switched off. Luckily, we were all together, with Darren asleep under the purple blanket and me reading my Ned Kelly book while Ma sorted through our washing.

When the lights flicked off, I cried out. I don't really like the dark that much.

Ma said it was probably just a blown fuse because old houses always have problems with wires and stuff. But I had a weird, scared feeling, like this was something bad. I went out with her to the front of the house to hold the torch so she could check the fuse box. But it wasn't just one blown fuse. It was all the fuses. They were gone. Someone had taken them. Every single one!

Ma closed the box without saying anything and just marched back into the house and upstairs with the torch, making sure I was following her. When we got back to our room, Ma locked the door and sat with her back to it, Darren's cricket bat nestled across her knees.

I don't think she slept a wink the whole night because she was in the exact same position when I woke up this morning.

18 NOVEMBER 1973

Things have been getting worse. Men have been outside our house every night, yelling and throwing rocks at our windows. Ma sits guard at our door, watching and holding that cricket bat. Then last night we heard the men break in downstairs and smash a lot of stuff.

I was terrified they would come up to our room and I think Ma was too because she made Darren and I hide in the closet. But the men stayed downstairs, laughing and drinking and calling out Ma's name until almost dawn.

When the goons finally left, we all went downstairs to see how much damage they had done. The place was a complete wreck. All the downstairs windows were smashed, doors kicked in. Ma told us we weren't to go out of her sight, so we all stayed in and cleaned up the mess.

I asked her why we didn't call the cops and she shook her head and said the cops weren't going to be any help. Then she just carried on sweeping up the glass and plaster that was all over the floor.

We need someone to help us though, because those goons are not going to give up until they force us out.

I know that now.

I saw them all day, passing by our window or standing across the road laughing at us as we swept and cleaned and tossed things away. Pickaxe himself turned up and stuck his head through our broken front window while I was in the front room sweeping up the last of the glass. I looked up and there he was, like a monster from a storybook.

He startled me so much that I screamed really loudly and Ma came running from the kitchen and started hitting Pickaxe with the handle of her broom.

I have never seen her so angry or so violent. I don't think

Pickaxe was expecting it either and he backed out really quickly. He didn't go away, though, just stood a few feet back and talked to us casually, like he was just a neighbour popping over for a chat.

'Looks like you had a bit of trouble here,' he said, his tone light and teasing. Ma glared at him and called him a coward who liked frightening women and children but he didn't frighten her.

'These houses are protected by heritage orders. You can't knock 'em down. So just go and tell your boss to leave us all alone!' she told him.

Pickaxe nodded at this, but he didn't move away.

'Yeah, you're right, Missus,' he said instead. 'The houses are protected, but the people inside . . . I don't think there's anything the heritage people can do to protect you lot now, is there?'

I saw by the look on Ma's face that what Pickaxe said was true. A bunch of orders from some people in an office somewhere far away wasn't going to protect the likes of us.

'I'm here to make one last offer,' Pickaxe continued. 'I'll give you $250 and three train tickets to new digs out west. There's new government housing up there which will be cheaper than here. Safer too.'

Ma didn't answer, just rushed forward with the broom and gave him a mighty swipe through the window. You could have heard the thwack of it on his shoulder right up on Darlinghurst Road, I reckon.

'You get lost!' she yelled. 'You and your thugs and that bully landlord, Carson.'

Pickaxe backed away then, nursing his bruised shoulder and scowling. 'Don't say I didn't give you every chance to do this the easy way,' he muttered, before turning on his heel and swaggering up the street.

26 NOVEMBER 1973

It's been days of harassment now. The power is still off. But we have been using the bits of broken furniture and window frames and rubbish to keep a fire lit at night to give us light and a bit of heat. Thank goodness it's almost summer and warm enough that the drafty air coming through the house won't freeze us to death.

I'm in the house by myself at the moment, which I'm not supposed to be. Harry's offered Ma a couple of daytime shifts and she couldn't turn them down, so she dropped us off at Mick's before she left. I was worried about the house being empty and unprotected, so I snuck back here to keep watch. The thugs don't usually bother us during the daytime, anyway.

Hang on, I think I hear a noise downstairs . . .

27 NOVEMBER 1973

We are all at Mick's house now. Something really bad has happened!

That noise I heard wasn't just some thug throwing a random brick. It was a whole bunch of thugs breaking in! Pickaxe was at the front, breaking down our door with a sledgehammer and then throwing all the old downstairs furniture onto the street, in the rain, right in the middle of the day.

I tried to stop them, but I didn't stand a chance.

And then they were in our room, picking up our stuff and just flinging it out the door or out the window. Toys, clothes, Ma's washing basket. Everything. They even smashed the window open when our mattress wouldn't fit through the opening and threw it, blankets and all, right outside! I jumped up to try and save it, but there was nothing I could do. It just landed with a sickening wet thud right on the road!

People across the street came out to watch, but no-one offered to help, even when Pickaxe picked me up and dumped me right out on the street next to the old mattress.

I didn't know what else to do, so I ran up to Mick's house.

Mick wasn't there, but Jane and Lucy were in the house and they promised to send some blokes down to try and stop the thugs.

I wanted to get Ma. She would tell them what's what and get rid of them. Jane tried to stop me, saying I should stay there and get dry and stay safe, but I wasn't listening to her.

'Can you look after Darren?' I asked instead. 'And don't tell him what's happened. Not yet.'

Miss Jane said she would make sure Darren was all right and without even thanking her, I turned and ran down the Butler Stairs at breakneck speed, needing to get to Harry's and my ma as soon as I could. I knew if anyone could stop those thugs, she could.

I have never run so fast in my life. Down through the puddles and the rain, the stairs so slick and slippery that I fell down quite a few times. But I just jumped back up and kept running. You don't grow up around Butler Stairs without learning how to recover from a fall!

With no time to lose, I hobbled on, gaining speed as I got used to the pain in my arms and knees.

When I got to Harry's Cafe de Wheels, I could barely speak, but Ma knew something was wrong the moment she saw me and she dropped everything and raced for home.

Outside our house, it was chaos. The Push and the thugs were having a right old blue as Ma and I got there. Number 85 was partially boarded up now. All our possessions dumped on the street, not even packed up or anything. Even the cheap furniture that the Gattos had left was broken or abandoned on the street and our mattress and our purple blanket were covered with mud and tyre marks where thugs in their cars had driven over them rather than swerve to avoid the obstruction.

A pale blue police car had pulled up, its sirens blaring, and Jane's men and Pickaxe's thugs started to pull away from each other. A few fists were still being thrown as the cops ran up and started grabbing the members of the Push.

I saw pretty quickly that they weren't even interested in the men who had been removing our stuff. They were only arresting the people who were trying to help us!

Mick arrived and asked my ma if she had signed anything or taken any money. She hadn't, so Mick tried to tell the cops it was an illegal eviction, but they wouldn't listen.

Eventually, one of the coppers told Mick that he should go down to the cop shop to sort it out. But Ma looked too scared and exhausted to do anything, so Mick took us back to his flat and we were reunited with Darren.

We are sleeping in their back room for tonight.

Ma says she is going to sort it all out with the coppers tomorrow because our rent is paid and they had no right to do what they did!

28 NOVEMBER 1973

I insisted on going down to the cop shop with Jane and Ma today.

I was a witness and could tell them exactly how those goons had broken into our house and taken everything that wasn't theirs.

The copper behind the desk wasn't very friendly and said I had to sit down and be quiet while he spoke to Ma.

So, Jane and I sat back in the plastic chairs in the waiting area, watching Ma try to explain the situation to this mean-faced old copper.

'Sounds like you were legally evicted, ma'am,' he said pompously, refusing to look my red-faced, furious mother in the eye.

'I told you I didn't sign anything. There was no final eviction notice. I paid my rent. They had no right!' my ma replied, trying not to lose her temper completely. 'I want to talk to the sergeant, there has been a mistake here.'

The policeman looked grumpy at this but made a phone call and soon a big man with steel-grey hair appeared in the waiting room with us. I recognised him as the man who had threatened to arrest Mrs Fowler when she had been thrown out by the thugs. I didn't think he was going to help us much and I was right.

'We have been in contact with your landlord, Mrs Krum,' he said, not even offering her a seat or anything, just standing in front of her and looking at my ma the way Mrs Garth looks at the kids who are naughty in the playground.

'Our eviction notice is before the courts. They have no right to remove us until it is heard.'

'Well, the landlord says he does have a signed termination

of lease from the leaseholder.'

'I never signed anything!' Ma insisted,

'No, you didn't,' the sergeant agreed, 'but your husband did.'

Ma stepped back, the surprise clear on her face. 'My husband? Wilhelm?' She shook her head. 'He doesn't live with us.'

'That may be,' the sergeant said. 'But he is the registered leaseholder and he signed a termination of the lease.'

'But he's not the resident. Surely that's invalid,' Jane said then as my ma backed away and sat, white-faced, on the chair beside me.

'He doesn't have to be the resident. Just the leaseholder. That's the law,' the copper said smugly. 'Now, you're wasting police time. This is an issue between that woman and her husband. Not a police matter.'

'But we have nowhere to go,' Ma said softly. 'All our stuff is still lying on the street. I . . . I . . .'

This was the first time I had seen my ma lost for words and it scared me more than a bunch of thugs ever could.

'Well, that's not our problem, ma'am,' the sergeant said, turning to go. 'Perhaps you should use the payout to get a hotel or something.'

'Payout?' Ma said.

The sergeant sighed and gave Ma a look like she was a piece of dirt on the bottom of his shoe.

'Mr Carson said he paid your husband fifty dollars in compensation, as required by law. That is all there is to it. You need to find somewhere else to go. It's all perfectly legal.'

He turned and I saw Miss Jane's hand shoot out and grab the copper by the elbow, pinching his arm and making him face her.

She leaned in, inches from the sergeant's wrinkled, ugly mug.

'You know what is going on in that street. The threats, the intimidation. Women and children, old ladies. Thrown out of their own homes! And you just sit there taking your cut, doing nothing. You're a disgrace!'

The sergeant pulled away and said she was lucky he didn't arrest her right there and then for assaulting a police officer, but that he wouldn't because she was obviously hysterical.

29 NOVEMBER 1973

We are moving into the house at number 57. There are already a bunch of squatters there, including my friend Jennie and her mum, and Mick reckons we should be safe for a few months at least.

I asked if number 57 had the lights on and Mick gave me a funny old look.

'How long have you three been living without power?' he asked. Ma's face reddened.

'Just a few days.'

'Oh hell, we should have helped you a lot sooner. I'm sorry, Elena.'

Ma pulled away from him and said we could look after ourselves, but there were tears in her eyes and I knew she was exhausted. None of us had slept much for days. I don't think my ma had slept at all.

Mick didn't say anything, he just put his arms around my mother and hugged her fiercely. Ma wasn't expecting that and didn't think to push him away.

'We all need other people sometimes, Elena. We are weakest when we are on our own and strongest when we stick together. And we should have stuck by you sooner. But we are going to make sure you are okay from now on.'

Ma nodded and hugged Mick right back. I think she may have been crying then, but she hid her face so I couldn't be sure. I think this was the first time I had ever seen my ma just relax and stop fighting so hard.

And I was glad.

30 NOVEMBER 1973

Our new home.

Number 57 Victoria Street is pretty much exactly the same as our old house—crumbling, run-down, but still somehow kind of grand.

The house is set out on two levels. There's a narrow hallway down the middle leading to a set of narrow wooden stairs and there's a big kitchen in the back. Coming off the hallway are two doorways, but there are no doors here. Instead, the rooms are set up as a big common room where all the people who are living in the house can come and hang out together on big brown couches and red beanbags.

The floor is covered in the same brown swirly carpet that

we had in our old house and it has the exact same stickiness and moist squishing sound when you walk on it. Even the blooms of mould on the downstairs walls look familiar.

But this house, unlike ours, is bursting at the seams with people. Sitting on couches or on the floor, laughing, chatting, making cups of tea or dancing to the music that plays constantly on the record player in the common room.

More long-haired men and short-haired women were sitting on the stairs or leaning up against the walls of the hallway as we came in. The glorious, bubbling noise of all these strange people was comforting and familiar after the emptiness and isolation of our old place.

We soon settled in. We even got the same room on the first floor that we had in our old house, although this room had three single mattresses instead of our old, big double one and my purple blanket was nowhere to be seen. I guess no-one felt like picking it up, all soggy and nasty from the middle of the road. I missed the purple blanket, though, because we'd had that for as long as I could remember.

Despite the loss of our mattress and my blanket, I am happy for the first time in days. Really, properly happy. Everyone here is so upbeat. They are always smiling and joking and there's always someone with a story to tell or a song to sing. Plus Jennie is just across the hall, so we can hang out all the time now. I even saw Ma smiling a couple of times when she didn't think I was looking.

I also made another friend here, a boy called Fred who is kind of quiet, but handsome and funny like Tony was. I think we might even have the makings of a whole new Vic Street gang right here in this house.

2 DECEMBER 1973

Most of the people who came into Victoria Street at the start of the year to protest have given up by now. The only ones left are the more battle-hardened students of the Push, a few of our old neighbours and some people who have come in from outside the area, mostly writers and artists like Jennie and Fred's folks. There's only about twenty of us left in all the Carson houses now.

The street has a weird, empty feeling. Especially when you pass the boarded-up buildings that used to be filled with friends and neighbours. The thugs leave the houses we are in more or less alone, but they are always stealing things and breaking into the other abandoned places. They also love hassling us all when we're out on the street.

7 DECEMBER 1973

Jennie, Fred, Darren and I have taken to wandering up to Mr Botticelli's shop once or twice a day, not as a proper street patrol like the adults do, but just to report on any shenanigans the thugs might be up to.

Ma said that was all right as long as we didn't do anything stupid like confront a vandal or get into a blue with anyone. We were just to watch and report anything that was happening.

We never see much, just a few goons standing around the corners giving us the hairy eyeball or cruising up and down Vic Street in their hotted-up Commodores and Ford Falcons.

They always look really stupid when they get to the William Street end. It's been blocked off for months because of the roadworks for the new highway, so they have to turn those big stupid cars around, which takes ages. Darren and Fred and Jennie and I stand on the pavement nearby jeering at them and telling them they are going to hit a tree or something, so they have to brake really sharply, even though they have miles of room.

8 DECEMBER 1973

Things have changed in the street. There's more graffiti and the patrols have found loads of smouldering mattresses in the empty houses. Luckily, they were found and put out before they turned into full-on fires.

Dossers are sleeping in some of the empty houses so it's hard to tell if they are lighting the fires to cook with or if the thugs are doing it, but if you ask me, I bet it's Pickaxe and his goons—who would cook anything over a flaming mattress?

Luckily, there hasn't been another big house fire since May, but I think they might be starting to get really bold now. Mick says to be on our guard and watch for anything suspicious.

12 DECEMBER 1973

Yesterday was the scariest day of my whole entire life!

I can hardly believe it all happened, but it did.

I was with Jennie and Darren and Fred and we were walking back from the shop like we did most days after school, just keeping an eye out, you know. We hadn't seen anything funny on our way up to the shop and so we were pretty relaxed coming back, talking about the Irish stew we were expecting to eat for dinner at the squat. Then suddenly Darren stopped in the middle of the road and announced that there were ghosts in our old house. He pointed to number 85, which was still all boarded up and seemed quiet enough to me. I thought maybe he was imagining something, although Darren isn't usually one to make things up. Then I heard it, too. Someone moving around inside the house.

We went a bit closer and saw that two of the boards had been pulled off the downstairs window. Someone had obviously pushed their way inside.

'Maybe it's just some old dossers,' Jennie said.

None of us really wanted to go inside because it could be drunks or the goons or someone else really nasty, so we decided just to go and tell the others about it.

But then we heard it. The sound of laughter. Kids' laughter.

The laughter was followed by some loud shouting, more laughter and then the unmistakable sound of spray paint.

These weren't some dossers or a pack of goons. They were just kids, and I was pretty sure we could scare away a few kids.

Jennie thought we should go and tell Mick, but I was mad now. This was my house. Okay, I might not live in it right now, but that is because we can't fix the power. That didn't mean I was going to let some little ratbags go in there and mess it up even more.

Without thinking, I clambered up onto the windowsill and was inside the darkened house within moments. In the gloom, I almost tripped on the debris and garbage that was scattered across the floor. I picked my way through it carefully, seeing the spill of the torchlights and hearing the kids talking in the back, near the kitchen. It was still light outside, but all the boarded-up windows made it gloomy and dark in there. Luckily, I knew this place like the back of my hand and would have been able to find my way to the kitchen even if it had been pitch-dark.

I heard someone fall in through the window behind me and I turned to see Jennie. She cursed as she stood up and dusted herself off. Fred followed just behind her, slightly less noisily.

I saw my brother's ghostly face appear at the window, looking like he, too, was going to follow us in. I quickly told him to run and get Mick or someone from the Push, as quick as he could. Darren gave me a thumbs-up and ran off down the street. I turned back to the kitchen doorway, Jennie and Fred in step behind me.

Whoever was in there had obviously heard our entrance and there was much muffled, worried whispering and scurrying about as we walked through.

One of the kids pointed a torch directly at my face, blinding me as he ran forwards, attempting to tackle me to the ground. Jennie dodged to the side, but Fred jumped forwards, taking the kid down and knocking the torch from his hand.

Good work, Fred!

It took me a few moments to regain my vision and by that time all hell had broken loose.

There were four vandals, older teenage boys, and they did not like that we had disturbed them. They were yelling and throwing bits of wood and plaster at us. We did our best to duck and nothing too hard hit us, but we had to shield our eyes and heads so we heard but didn't see them run past us and scamper out the window.

I thought they were all gone until I heard someone moving in the kitchen, still smashing and breaking things. Jennie and Fred hung back but I pulled open the kitchen door and stepped inside. There was a boy about my age kicking in the kitchen cabinets. I yelled for him to stop and he turned to face me.

I would have known that face anywhere.

Tommo Jenkins.

And of course, he knew me.

'Billie No Mates!' he said jeeringly. 'What are you doing here?'

'I'm here to stop you,' I said.

Tommo just laughed and pulled out a box of matches from his pocket, quickly lighting one and tossing it into a pile of rags and the wood he had pulled off the kitchen cupboards. He had every intention of burning the whole house down.

As I watched, the small match exploded into a bigger flame as the rags and wood and rubbish caught fire. Tommo laughed and pushed past me, making his escape.

I didn't even care about him now. I had to put the flames out. I had to save my house.

I ran at the fire, trying to stamp out the rags. Amazingly, the flames started to die down. I saw Jennie peering in the doorway and yelled at her and Fred to run and get help. She hesitated for a moment and then disappeared.

I kept stamping; there were just a few rags on fire now. I was going to do this. I was going to put the fire out.

Then I heard another **WHOOSH** and saw flames burning out in the hallway. Tommo had lit another fire on his way out. From outside the window, Jennie and Fred were screaming for me to get out. They were right. If I didn't get out now, I would be trapped. I had no choice, so I ran out the kitchen door and into the flaming hallway, using Fred and Jennie's voices to lead me through the smoke to the gap in the front window. I was almost there when I heard someone crying for help behind me. I turned and saw a dark figure standing on the top of the stairs. He was hard to see in all the smoke, even as the light from the fire was raging. Some old dosser, probably taking shelter in the house. Maybe he was the one who had prised off the boards on the window which allowed Tommo and his mates a way to get in?

Even if it was his fault, I couldn't just leave the man there.

'I'm down here,' I yelled. 'Just keep walking directly forwards but be careful, the stairs are really steep.'

But the man just stood there, like a statue, on the top of the steps. I didn't hesitate, just ran up the stairs and took the man's hand, ready to lead him down the stairs before we were both burned to death.

'Wilomena?' the man asked, surprised.

I looked up at him and realised it was my father.

'Come on,' I shouted, 'we have to get out of here!'

'I was just sleeping,' Pa said. 'I had nowhere else to go.'

'Come on, we have to hurry,' I replied, guiding my father down the stairs. He was unsteady on his feet and had to hold the handrail to stop from falling, but we got to the bottom and I could see the window up ahead.

Jennie was standing just outside the window, but I couldn't get to her. The fire had cut off me and my Pa.

'Get out of here, Jennie!' I yelled. She hesitated, but there was nothing she could do. She had no way to put out the fire and if she didn't leave, she would be burned alive, too. My father clutched at my hand and looked me in the eye.

'I'm sorry, Billie girl. So sorry.'

I had waited my whole life for him to say that to me, but now I realised it didn't matter. It was all too late. Everything was over now. No point being angry about anything he did or didn't do. I wondered if I had known it was him, would I have gone up and saved him? And I realised I would. No matter what, I wouldn't have left anyone to die, not even him.

'Billie! Billie!' A voice cried out in the smoke. It was Darren, his voice thin and scared, echoing from the front rooms.

'Stay out there!' I screamed, beside myself with terror now. Even if I couldn't save myself, I had to keep Darren safe.

'Billie!' a deeper, older voice called.

Mick!

'Mick! Mick, we're in here!' I screamed, my voice hoarse with fear and smoke. 'Help us, we're trapped.'

There were other voices then. Lots of them. And through the haze I saw people and heard the splashing of water as buckets and watering-cans and saucepans and anything else that could hold water was thrown onto the flames.

As soon as the fire allowed, Ma and Mick and Wanda were there, carrying me and my pa out. All of us spluttering and coughing and then drinking in the clean, cool outside air.

Fred, Darren and Jennie were sitting together on a parked car and they looked relieved as they saw me being brought out. A dark-eyed woman passed me a mug filled with water and I drank it down greedily, spluttering and almost choking on the liquid as it rushed down my raw, painful throat.

Its cold comfort did ease the pain a bit, though.

I saw Tommo Jenkins standing on the curb, held by two men from the Sydney Push. He looked pale and terrified, even while his face was black with soot and dust. I jumped up and ran over to him, shoving him backwards.

'Why did you do that!'

He shook his head dumbly. 'They paid me five dollars,' he said, still not looking at me. 'I didn't know anyone was in there, the houses are supposed to be empty.'

'You saw me in there and you lit another fire anyway,' I said, furious now. 'Why can't you all just leave us alone? Why do they have to destroy everything?'

'Because they want you out,' he answered, looking at me with dull, lifeless eyes. 'And blokes like them are used to getting what they want.'

Then tears sprang to his eyes and I saw that he was scared and ashamed, realising the seriousness of what he had done and what had almost happened to me.

18 DECEMBER 1973

My pa disappeared after the fire. I don't know where he went. Someone said they saw him taking a train out west, but no-one knows for sure. I am not sorry he's gone. I'm not sorry I saved him, either.

Turned out Tommo was right about the thugs, too. They were not going to give up. And over the last few days several other houses have been broken into. Patrols found smouldering mattresses, rags, graffiti and sledgehammered walls everywhere. It's dangerous to even enter most of the abandoned houses now, in case the roofs cave in. It seems like whatever has been holding the thugs back is gone now and it's on for young and old.

Ma has forbidden me to go out after dark and I am not allowed to enter any of the abandoned houses for any reason. I don't mind. I think I am happy staying out of them, at least for a while.

Yet as terrible as it has become, the people in our squat seem to have become merrier and the house is always filled with singing and dancing, painting and writing.

We even made up a song about it all called 'The Struggles of Vic Street' and it's become our nightly singalong. I think

I might enter it into the Prime Minister's National Anthem competition because it is way better than anything else I have come up with and it really is about the true Aussie spirit.

More people have arrived, too, and the house has swelled again. I am watching Ma carefully every day, looking to see if there is any hint that she is ready to give up and get us all out before things get too bad.

So far, she seems like she is in it to the end, just like me.

22 DECEMBER 1973

It's two days before Christmas Eve and Mick visited us today at number 57 and called a house meeting.

Everyone gathered together. There are more people living in the house now, though I don't know all of them because a lot of them move in and out, staying only for a few days before moving on and being replaced by other students or hippies. There are still a few of us old timers, though. Old Mr Stanislav, who used to live down the street, lives in the basement flat and spends most of his time writing letters to the Sydney papers trying to tell them how bad it is getting here on Victoria Street.

Although we check the papers every day, we have never seen them publish even one of his letters to the editor. There is another writer here, too—Woody, who is a proper journalist and his stories have been published in one of the big Sydney papers, which is pretty awesome. And my mates Jennie and Fred and their mums are still here. Like us, they reckon they are staying for as long as it takes to win. So, when Mick came around everyone gathered in the front room listening with rapt attention as he explained what was happening.

'We lost our last possible court case,' he said, 'which means we can now be legally evicted from the houses, at any time. We've only got this one, number 59 and my house with anyone in it, so it won't be hard for them to target us. They are going to come for us soon. So, we have a choice. We can give up, leave quietly and let them have the houses, or we can dig in and fight.'

Everyone in the house looked around nervously and Ma hugged Darren close. But no-one said anything.

Mick told us that the squatters in the other house had decided to hold on and they were preparing for the thugs by boarding up their windows and barricading the doors.

Jennie's mum asked if that would keep the thugs out and Mick just shrugged. 'Maybe for a few days . . . or a week,' he said.

'What's the point?' Mr Stanislav asked wearily.

'The papers will cover this,' Woody said. 'If they try to barge in all guns blazing while there are still women and children here, it will make news.'

'Yeah,' one of the new university students agreed. 'The Battle of Victoria Street. It might be what we need to get the public on side again. We've lost a lot of ground since Jack Mundey lost the leadership of the BLF. That new guy, Gallagher, he's already told us he won't hold the up the green ban, so the union can't refuse to drive the bulldozers or tear down the houses anymore. All we've got is heritage orders on a few houses and they aren't backed by any laws or anything. We need people to come out and see that what is happening here is not right and stand with us.'

Mick took a gulp of his coffee and looked at me and Darren and Jennie and Fred. 'There are kids here, though, and it will be dangerous. Everyone has to make their own decision, we are not going to force anyone to stay,' he said.

Ma nodded and I knew she was thinking that we should just leave. I had to do something, so I stepped forwards and I spoke up. Not too loudly at first because I was really scared. I don't think anyone even realised I was speaking, but Mick heard me and he told everyone to be quiet and listen.

‘I just want to say,’ I began. Ma tried to pull me into her arms, but I really needed to tell them all how I felt, how much this meant to me, so I struggled away and stood in the centre of the room.

‘I’ve been reading about Ned Kelly,’ I told them all, ‘and this is like Kelly’s last stand. We can’t just give up. We all have to show them that they can’t bully us and get away with it. We will show them that we won’t go down without a fight.’

‘Kelly lost, kid,’ Woody reminded me.

I turned to him and nodded. ‘Yeah, he did. But he became famous anyway. He’s the one people think is the hero. Not those coppers who surrounded and outnumbered him. Not the rich landowners who tried to steal everything from him. Because he fought, we all know what happened to him. And people need to know what is happening here. Maybe they won’t care now, but maybe in the future people will see what we did here and it will inspire them to fight against injustice, just like Ned Kelly inspires us. We can’t let them win.’

The room went quiet and I could see my ma was looking at me and smiling.

Mick was smiling, too. ‘Well, damn, kid,’ he said. ‘I couldn’t have said it better myself.’

So, we are staying. All of us.

CHRISTMAS DAY 1973

Today was the best Christmas I can remember.

Everyone in number 57 chipped in and bought a bunch of new records.

I used my savings to buy Ma the new Helen Reddy single, 'I Am Woman' and she loved it so much she played it over and over again, singing at the top of her lungs. And with what was left over, I went up to the souvenir shop on Darlinghurst Road and bought Darren that stupid snow globe he was always looking at in the shop window. It's a silly piece of plastic really, and the Sydney skyline is painted really badly in the background. But I think the words in the snow globe are pretty perfect right now: I wish I lived in Darlinghurst, Sydney.

Well, we do. At least for now, anyway.

Darren and I got new clothes from the charity shop. Darren got a pair of blue denim overalls and a green T-shirt and I got a pair of purple paisley corduroy jeans with bell-bottom flares. They look almost new and I have worn them nonstop since I got them.

After we unwrapped the pressies, everyone started painting pictures of ourselves along the hallway wall. I think one of the university students started the idea, saying that we should have something to remember the day by and it didn't matter what we did to the walls if the house was going to be knocked down anyway. Usually, Ma would never have let us draw on the walls like that, but even she was joining in. I think we all knew this was our last chance to make our mark here.

My ma is a surprisingly good artist and she drew a great picture of me and Darren and her all standing together holding hands. I am not quite so good and my picture of Mr Stanislav didn't really look like him at all. So then I had the idea of everyone dipping their hands in paint and putting their handprint next to their portraits and signing them. Everyone agreed it was a bonza idea.

We got a lot of paint everywhere, but it was loads of fun.

I added a portrait of Susie and Tony the Cat so they could be with us in spirit.

I sent Susie and Tony some Christmas cards—but I never got any in return. It's not surprising because the thugs stole all the mailboxes from all the houses weeks ago.

28 DECEMBER 1973

Word came through today.

Something is going to happen soon.

We have spent all day barricading the doors and windows and filling up the cupboards to prepare for a siege. Mick and the members of the Push have told anyone who wants to get out they must go before everything is completely boarded up.

I saw Ma packing up our things and I thought she was going to make us all leave, even though she had promised we could stay, right until the end. But when I asked her, she said it was just in case, because if things did go bad, she wanted to be able to get out fast, but we would stay until it was not safe to stay anymore.

I love my ma and am glad that I am fearless just like her.

30 DECEMBER 1973

After all that excitement, nothing actually happened.

It's quieter than ever and the patrols are coming back saying that the thugs aren't even on the street anymore.

Maybe we won. Maybe they realised we were not going to give up and decided to stop and go pick on someone else.

1 JANUARY 1974

I'm twelve today.

Almost a grown-up.

There's still nothing happening on the street and number 57 looks kind of silly all boarded up with mattresses against all the windows. It's really hot in here as well.

At least we took the boards off the front door yesterday so we can all sit out on the pavement in the evening and stay cool. It's going to be another really hot summer.

Last night, for New Year's Eve, we lit firecrackers out on the street and then Ma took us up to Fitzroy Gardens to see the lights and all the people singing in the new year.

Darren and I ran all the way there, carrying our sparklers. We didn't quite make it in time for the New Year countdown, so we started singing 'Auld Lang Syne' as we walked up Darlo Road. An American soldier gave my ma a big pash! She was so embarrassed, but she was smiling too.

And Darren and I got to stay up until after midnight!

Everyone here is relaxed and it looks like everything is going to be all right in Victoria Street now.

No-one knows why exactly, but maybe the thugs and Pickaxe man and the mean landlord saw the papers which called them greedy and decided to make a New Year's resolution to be better and stop bullying people. Ma says she is going to try to get her shifts back at Harry's now that everything has settled down.

Later, we are going to the city. Ma is taking me out to have a special birthday lunch at the cafe at the very top of Woolworths on Pitt Street and everyone from the house is going to come along. It's my favourite restaurant in the whole world and I am going to order the deep-fried lambs' brains which taste like melting clouds in my mouth when I bite into them.

Darren won't eat the brains, so he'll have sausages and, if we are good, Ma will let us share an ice cream sundae with chocolate topping.

1974 is going to be the best year ever!

3 JANUARY 1974

I was so wrong. The thugs didn't give up at all! They are coming, right now! We heard the men breaking in about twenty minutes ago.

Ma is making us leave so I don't have much time to write. I will fill this all in later to make sure I remember everything that went down.

4 JANUARY 1974

We got out yesterday.

The men came at about 7 am.

Thugs and coppers. Loads of them.

It took them hours to break through the barricades.

Some of the men in our house climbed up on the roof. There's one still sitting on the chimney stack today. The coppers tried to get him down by putting a fire in the fireplace, but he just used a blanket to cover the top of the chimney and it was the coppers who had to run outside, coughing and spluttering.

Ma, Darren and I stayed inside for as long as we could, but when the thugs broke through the walls, Ma got us all outside really quickly. We stayed on the street till it got dark, though, chanting and singing. Ma even spoke to one of the TV people who were swarming about with their television cameras.

I told one of the newspaper men that I'd just celebrated my birthday and he laughed and said it would be one to remember. I guess he's right.

7 JANUARY 1974

The battle for Victoria Street is finally over. The last of the protesters have been arrested or have given up. Three days they held out, which I think is pretty amazing, but in the end, we lost.

I guess we knew we were going to.

Doesn't feel any better, though.

We are now staying in a boarding house until Ma finds us somewhere more permanent to live. She couldn't get her job back at Harry's, so she's gone out to see if there are any waitressing or retail jobs around. We don't have much of our stuff. Most of it was left behind or broken when we ran out of number 57, although I made sure I grabbed Darren's snow globe. It's a bit cracked from where I dropped it, but it still has all its snow.

I pick it up all the time and swirl the snow around, watching the little flakes settle after the flurry of action and chaos when I shake it up. Seeing it all return to normal no matter how hard I shake it makes me feel better somehow. Reading the words in the globe makes me sad, though. I wish I lived in Darlinghurst. It is a funny thing for tourists to take away with them because they could never know what it is really like living there. How great the people are, and how you could sit under the shade of the big trees and do nothing much but still have the best day because you were with all your mates and you were in your home.

That's all gone now. Because we lost. It's going to be a carpark or maybe an office block soon and maybe then a freeway or a train station or whatever else the developers decide to do with it now they have got all us ratbags out. And no-one will ever get to live in number 85 Victoria Street ever again.

8 JANUARY 1974

The news reports are full of what happened at Vic Street. People are siding with us, not the coppers or the thugs, so maybe we did win—a little bit, anyway. Ma said Carson had to go back to court and the houses are staying up. At least for now.

Whatever happened, we can't go back to Victoria Street. All the houses are boarded up now and the people on the rest of the street hate us for all the drama that unfolded, even though it wasn't our fault. I don't know where we will go, but the Victoria Street that was my home has gone now. There's no getting it back.

AUGUST 1976

I just found this old journal. I had totally forgotten about how much I had written in it.

All that stuff about Vic Street and what happened there seems so long ago, but it was only a few years.

I don't know why I stopped writing in this journal. I guess got too busy. We have moved so much since we left Vic Street.

It's hard to find anywhere we can stay permanently, so we have lived in three flats and three boarding houses in two years. Each time we moved on because it wasn't safe or because Ma couldn't afford the rents as they rose higher and higher. We had to go on the waiting list for government housing, and it seemed like we waited forever, but we finally got our very own flat a few weeks ago. It's in Surry Hills, which is only a few suburbs away from Darlinghurst, but it feels a million miles away. It's okay here but there are no trees, no Dandelion Fountain, no Butler Stairs. No Jennie or Susie or Fred or Tony. Just me and Darren stuck in the flat all day when we aren't at school. We go to a school in Redfern now, so I don't even get to see Mrs Frater or any of the kids from Plunkett Street anymore. I have started to make some new friends, but it's not the same, and I am always worried we will be run out of here, too. I don't want to have to lose another load of friends, so I am trying not to get too close to anyone.

Ma reckons we can stay here at least until I finish high school, because it's owned by the government and the rent is fixed. But I remind her that the houses in Woolloomooloo and The Rocks were owned by the government, too, and nothing stopped the government tossing those people out until Jack Mundey and the BLF came and put in the green ban.

There's no such thing as a green ban anymore. Jack Mundey is gone and the BLF doesn't try to stop any development now. So, if the government decides it wants to build a road here, or a carpark or whatever, well, now there's no-one to stop them.

At least I still have Darren, who is just as kind and sweet as he always was. I think he misses Vic Street, too, because I often see him playing with his little snow globe, staring at that painted skyline, and I imagine he is thinking about how we used to look out our window and see the real thing just below.

Sometimes on the weekend when Ma is working, I take Darren on the bus down to Darlinghurst and we go and visit our old street. But it's very different now.

Mick is still there, still in number 115, still fighting eviction orders and working to save what's left of the street. But there are no members of the Push around anymore and Mrs Fowler died a little while back, so Mick seems awfully alone there.

I tried to visit Miss Jane a few times, but she wasn't home and no-one knew where she was.

When I asked Mick about her, he wouldn't say anything, just said that she would be so proud of me and that he hopes that I remember how important it is to fight for fairness, even if we lose.

He said I taught him that. Me and Ned Kelly.

He might be right, but we didn't completely lose the fight because most of the houses are still standing. Turns out the heritage people did manage to save a lot of them after all because of how important and historical this place is. I bet that made Mr Carson really, really mad!

I'm happy that our old house at number 85 is still standing.

Maybe one day we'll be able to move back there, Ma and Darren and me. I miss it, but not just because of the house. I miss the people. Mr and Mrs Gatto and their Italian food. Tony the Cat and Susie, Mrs Fowler and her lace doilies, the brave women of the Sydney Push who looked so cool and sophisticated and made me believe I could be as elegant as them one day.

I even miss Mr Botticelli and the mean landlady who ran the boarding house across the road. And Mrs Finnegan and all the Finnegan kids, splashing around and making a mess. I miss going down to the Loo and I miss Plunkett Street and Mrs Frater and all the kids I used to know there.

But most of them are gone now, too, and the street doesn't seem the same because a place isn't just about buildings and streets and shops, it's about the people who live there. And all the people I knew are gone.

I don't think Victoria Street is my home anymore now. But at least, thanks to us, other people might get to live in my house one day. They will have new adventures and new friends and new experiences, all because people in our street fought to save it.

People might say we lost the battle of Victoria Street, but I reckon it's better to say that Mr Carson didn't win. He never got to put up his office buildings or his carpark and the houses are still there for other kids to live in. And we never gave into the bullies. That's the real victory, I reckon.

HISTORICAL NOTES

On 3 January 1974, armed police, local thugs and paid strongmen forcibly broke into several houses in Victoria Street, Sydney. The houses were occupied by women and children as well as activists and students who had moved in to try to help protect the houses from demolition. This action became known as the Siege of Victoria Street and was the last great battle in the green ban struggles of the 1970s.

'Green ban' was the term used by the Builders' Labourers' Federation (BLF), led by union leader, Jack Mundey. It referred to the BLF's decision not to supply labourers and construction workers to any development site where residents were being forcibly evicted, or where heritage or public space was to be destroyed by development. Successful green bans in Kelly's Bush, The Rocks, Woolloomooloo and Centennial Park were supported by the local residents in each suburb and later by political activists like the Sydney University group, the Sydney Push. This resulted in residents being able to stay in their homes and avoid forced evictions, as well as the preservation of historical buildings and natural habitats for wildlife around the harbour area. Prior to the green ban movement, there was no heritage or environmental legislation at all in New South Wales or anywhere in Australia. Very few legislators were actually interested in heritage as an issue

The green bans, which ran from 1971 until 1975, were one of the most successful environmental and social justice campaigns Australia has ever seen. Thanks to the bravery of local residents and the BLF, previously unrestrained development now has to take into account the needs of both the environment and the working-class residents of Sydney City suburbs.

By the time the residents of Victoria Street began their fight in 1973, however, the power of the protesters and the unions was weakening. The landlord and developer of Victoria Street was alleged to have been complicit in many violent actions against the residents of the houses, including documented arson attacks and constant intimidation and harassment by hired thugs.

By the end of April 1973, most of the residents had been evicted from or left their homes in Victoria Street. Only a few hardened squatters continued to fight on, camping out in the houses scheduled for demolition. Many were university students, elderly residents or single mothers without the means or ability to move elsewhere. Those brave-hearted souls who stayed on faced months of threats, intimidation and violence in an effort to remove them from the thirty houses on Victoria Street which had been earmarked for a new office block and carpark development. On 6 January 1974, the final protester was removed and arrested, effectively ending the siege. The forces pitted against Victoria Street were the strongest faced during the green ban period and the bravery and determination of those who stayed and fought is particularly inspiring.

Even though many of the residents were removed after the siege, the struggle was not over. Residents and activists continued to fight the developer and others through the Australian courts and by supporting Heritage legislation. Eventually many of the buildings in Victoria Street were saved, although most of the residents were unable to return.

For more resources on the Green Ban Movement and the Siege of Victoria Street, please see these resources:

In print:

Green Bans, Red Unions: The Saving of a City by Meredith and Verity Burgmann (published by NewSouth Publishing, 2017).

Online:

Digital Classroom: https://digital-classroom.nma.gov.au/defining-moments/first-green-bans

The Greens: https://greens.org.au/about/green-bans

Jacobin: https://jacobin.com/2021/07/australia-sydney-urbanism-construction-builders-labourers-federation-nsw-green-labor-militancy

Libcom: https://libcom.org/article/list-green-bans-1971-1974

THE PEOPLE OF VICTORIA STREET

While Billie and her family, as well as many of the characters in this story, are fictitious, there were real people involved in the Victoria Street siege who are referred to in this book, including Mick Fowler, Jack Mundey and Reverend Ted Knoffs.

To find out more about the real people involved in the Green bans, please see this resource:

Green Bans 1971-Now: https://www.greenbans.net.au

TIMELINE OF THE GREEN BANS AND THE VICTORIA STREET BATTLES

March 1970 – A Sydney property developer starts buying up Victoria Street residences. By the end of 1971, he owns all the properties between and including numbers 55 and 115 Victoria Street.

June 1971 – After being approached by a group of concerned local residents, the BLF places the very first green ban on Kelly's Bush, a nature area in the Sydney suburb of Woolwich, guaranteeing that no site clearing or development will be undertaken by union workers in the area.

June 1971 – Development application to develop Victoria Street, Darlinghurst for office blocks and carparks is put to Sydney City Council.

Mid 1971 – Victoria Street residents request a green ban. BLF agree.

November 1971 – A green ban is placed on The Rocks area in Sydney after development plans are lodged for demolition of most residential homes.

December 1971 – Development application for Victoria Street is rejected.

February 1972 – The Congregational Church, now known as the Pitt Street Uniting Church, was placed under a green ban, saving it from proposed demolition.

March 1972 – The BLF places a green ban on the proposed Opera House Car Park construction due to its threat to Sydney's Royal Botanic Gardens. The ban is successful and the carpark is relocated to save the gardens.

June 1972 – A green ban is placed on the Theatre Royal in Sydney to prevent demolition. The building is saved and incorporated into new designs for the extended theatre before the ban is lifted.

June 1972 – The BLF imposes a green ban on the construction of a sporting complex and stadium in Sydney's Centennial Park. The park is saved.

Late 1972 – North-West Expressway gains a BLF green ban to prevent one-sixth of the total houses in Glebe and Balmain from being destroyed. The expressway is re-routed and all the residences, as well as the historic Glebe building 'Lyndhurst', are saved from demolition.

February 1973 – The BLF places a green ban on the Sydney suburb of Woolloomooloo. The green ban results in the end of violent bulldozing of houses in the area and negotiations which save sixty-five per cent of the public housing in the area from demolition.

March 1973 – The BLF extends a green ban on Victoria Street as demolition and development proposals continue to be lodged.

April-May 1973 – The Victoria Street Development application is approved by Council. Forced evictions begin.

April 8 1973 – The first official Victoria Street Action Group (VSAG) meeting is held.

11 April 1973 – The VSAG holds its second meeting at the Wayside Chapel, which was raided by thugs and police.

15 April 1973 – The BLF agrees to place another official green ban on Victoria Street after a request by the VSAG.

2 May 1973 – The National Trust officially classifies Victoria Street as heritage listed for reasons including its beauty and historical associations with major writers and artists.

14 May 1973 – A meeting between the developer and Victoria Street residents and BLF representatives is held, where agreement is made to cease all evictions and harassment until the final building plans are considered and agreed by the Heritage Trust. However, 'accidents' continue to be reported by residents, including mysterious fires being lit in empty houses, flash flooding in basement residences and reports of intimidation and harassment of female residents.

4 June 1973 – The Heritage Trust endorses the new development plan, which allows low-rise apartment buildings to be built on sites without heritage value. All historic housing facades would be retained.

10 June 1973 – A small group of squatters move into two of the empty houses—numbers 57 and 59—on Victoria Street. Soon other houses begin filling with squatters. All squatters pay rent: a quarter of their income up to a maximum of $10 a week.

June-July 1973 – Squatters and residents turn Mick Fowler's flat and the yard and garage of 115 Victoria Street into the centre for their resistance efforts, as well as a full-time daycare centre and crèche for residents and Victoria Street activists.

6 September 1973 – There is a fatal fire at number 103 Victoria Street. The cause remains unknown.

October 1973 – Norm Gallagher starts to challenge Jack Mundey as leader of the NSW chapter of the BLF, with an aim to stop and overturn the green bans.

16 October 1973 – Non-union labour is brought into The Rocks and begins demolishing buildings and residences in Playfair Street. In retaliation, four thousand BLF workers walk off all other construction sites in Sydney. Demolition of The Rocks is suspended.

3 December 1973 – Victoria Street squatter John Cox's appeal against his conviction for trespassing and being in a building without 'reasonable cause' is dismissed in the NSW Court. Squatting on Victoria Street is now officially illegal. Barricading of the Victoria Street houses begins.
29 December 1973 – The VSAG is told that police action is imminent and they should leave. The residents prepare for a showdown, but no cops appear.
3 January 1974 – The Siege of Victoria Street begins. It starts with an attack by police and thugs on number 57 Victoria Street at 7 am. By 8.30 am, almost all squatters have fled or been removed. Twenty-seven people are arrested for obstruction of police and twenty-six of them are placed in jail, along with thirteen supporters, mostly charged with obstruction. Two squatters remain defiant, Keith Mullins and Con Papadatos, both perching on the chimney at number 115.
4 January 1974 – Keith Mullins and Con Papadatos give up their protests and come down from number 115, however another squatter, known as Kipman, climbs up onto the neighbouring chimney to continue the protest.
5 January 1974 – Police arrest Kipman, removing him by demolishing the chimney around him. He is the last squatter to be removed from Victoria Street. The Siege of Victoria Street officially ends.
April 1974 – The NSW Heritage Trust begins the process of classifying the entire Rocks precinct in Sydney as an urban conservation area, permanently saving it from demolition and overdevelopment.
June 1974 – The NSW BLF is deregistered.
April 1975 – The green ban on Victoria Street is officially lifted by the new leadership of the BLF, almost two years after the ban was placed.
5 May 1976 – Mick Fowler, the last legal tenant, is evicted from his home in 115 Victoria Street after losing his last court appeal.